MACE!

This book is dedicated to the Beez

MACE!

James Grant

JAVELIN BOOKS

POOLE·NEW YORK·SYDNEY

First published in the UK by
Judy Piatkus (Publishers) Limited of London
This Javelin Books edition first published 1987
Javelin Books, Link House, West Street, Poole, Dorset, BH15 1LL

Distributed in Australia by
Capricorn Link (Australia) Pty Ltd,
PO Box 665, Lane Cove, NSW 2066

ISBN 0 7137 1994 X

Typeset by Phoenix Photosetting, Chatham
Printed and bound in Great Britain

This book is a work of fiction and all events described are entirely a product of the author's imagination. Some of the Los Angeles' establishments mentioned really exist, among them The Tail of the Cock and Carmelo's. The musicians who play there in this book: Johnny Guarnieri, Bob Florence, Nick Ceroli, Bob Cooper and Pete Christlieb are real people as are Bill Berry, his wife Betty, and their son Bill Jr. All other characters are entirely imaginary and any resemblance to any person living or dead is entirely coincidental. In the case of Helen Jerome and Lt. Bercovici this is a matter for regret.
Especially Lt. Bercovici.

Chapter One

The go-go dancer gyrated along the bar counter towards where I sat. I looked up, past her writhing hips and her heavy, swaying naked breasts and into her face. She could have been Mexican. She wasn't the girl I was looking for.

I stared down into my glass of whiskey and tried not to hear the remorseless pounding music that drowned out every other sound in the barroom.

The girl went past me and scrambled off the bar to disappear through a doorway in the back wall. I finished my drink, caught the bartender's eye and gestured for a refill. He slopped an inch into my glass and went back to reading the sports section of his newspaper. He had the face of a prizefighter, one who had taken too many punches. Scar tissue gave him a permanent frown, or maybe it's just that sportswriters use longer words these days.

I glanced around me. Maybe six or seven other punters had nothing better to do with their afternoons. The décor was strictly functional The lighting was what is known as discreet, which is another way of saying cheap. A man could die in one of the booths and no one need ever know.

Another girl was on the bar now. This one had painted her nipples with white Day-Glo and the flashing ultra-violet spotlight turned them into drunken fat fireflies. I looked at her face. I guessed she was eighteen. I did a mental sum. She was the sixty-seventh go-go girl I'd seen in maybe forty-eight hours. In the process I'd been inside more seedy bars than the average tourist knew even existed in Los Angeles.

The dancer came closer, I could see perspiration running in streams over her breasts from where it sprayed outwards. I put a protective hand over my whiskey glass. Soon her purple-painted toenails were right in front of me. They stayed there longer than her predecessor's had done. I leaned back and looked up at her round, muscular thighs and the rhinestone g-string which was all she wore. Sweat was forming there too and the black pubic hair sprouting around the g-string was shiny with it.

She was smiling down at me, a faintly desperate smile. I smiled back, only in sympathy. Now she didn't look a day over sixteen.

When she was off the bar she didn't go through the doorway right away, instead she looked back at me and winked. I turned away. The bartender was looking at me as well. His lean, tight face had all the expression of a stone statue of Buster Keaton.

The music had changed, still as loud, still as relentless in its deadening beat but my ears were in good enough shape to identify the tune as an old Ike and Tina Turner number done to death in an overarrangement for what sounded like a sixteen-piece rhythm section and only two horns.

There was a new girl on the bartop. She was slender and pretty. Blonde-haired and blue-eyed. I didn't look at her body because that wasn't why I was here. I was here because just before I left home in Liverpool, England, for a holiday in California one of my oldest friends had called up to ask if I would try to find his daughter who'd been in Los Angeles almost a year and hadn't written or telephoned home in the past six months.

I watched the blonde girl's face. I hadn't seen Linda Martin since she was six years old, just over ten years ago, but I had a fairly recent photograph of her in my wallet. There wasn't much doubt; number sixty-eight was the one I wanted. Just a few minutes friendly conversation and I could get on with the serious business of enjoying the first long holiday I'd had in years.

I waited a couple of minutes after she had gone through the doorway before I followed. The bartender watched me go but made no move to stop me. He had his newspaper to read, the half dozen morose drinkers to take care of. Besides which, he was smaller than me.

The doorway opened into a long narrow passageway with a single door down at the far end and another halfway along the left-hand wall. The walls and ceiling were painted in a shade of yellow that made my mouth go dry. The sound of the music was less oppressive back here but the beat still managed to reverberate through the confined space.

I was partway along the passage when a man came out of the doorway in the left-hand wall. He was the real reason why the bartender hadn't taken too much interest in me, for he was immense. Maybe he was an inch short of my six feet but he must have outweighted me by at least one hundred pounds. His huge gut almost filled the passageway as he leaned with his back against the door he closed behind him. I stopped a couple of paces short.

'Private,' he said through what appeared to be a mouth full of food. At least the spray of fine particles that blew from his mouth looked like breadcrumbs.

'I'm visiting one of the girls,' I told him politely.

'Oh yeah?'

'Yes.'

'Which one?'

'Linda.'

'Ain't no Linda. We gotta Michelle and a Lorelei and a Francoise and a Bettina but we ain't got no Linda.'

'Suppose I look for myself,' I suggested.

'Suppose you go fuck yourself,' he said.

I moved forward trying to figure a way past him, short of demolishing the building.

A gun appeared in his left hand. It happened so quickly and smoothly it must have been there all along but concealed by his bulk. He rested the barrel on his right forearm and looked at me in pleasure.

'Go ahead,' he said. 'Try something.'

I think he really wanted me to try; he needed an excuse to blow a hole in me the way some people need the next drink or another fix. I'd seen the signs before, every copper has, even one from Liverpool, and knew what to do. I froze.

He smiled widely, confirming that his mouth was full of food, and turned to face me. That was a mistake, not only did he give me a better target but it also meant he had to move the gun. As he was turning I shifted my balance onto my right foot and as he squared up to me I kicked him in the stomach with my left. Simultaneously, I slammed my right arm out forcing his gun hand up against the wall of the passage.

As his breath went out of his body, along with all the half-chewed food from his mouth, I picked the gun out of already nerveless fingers and removed the clip.

Lying on the floor, choking for breath, the fat man still represented an obstacle but one that was no longer insurmountable. I walked over him, using him as a combination bridge and doormat.

I slipped the gun and ammunition clip into my pockets as I went on down towards the end door. As I knocked on it the door opened and the Mexican girl came out. She looked at me in surprise, then past me along the passage.

'He's taking an early coffee-break,' I told her.

The Mexican girl grinned and went off to start her next show. She didn't need to climb over the fat man because she went through the door he'd come out of. I guessed that way led to the far end of the bar.

I rapped politely on the open door and went inside. The girl with the purple toenails was standing in the middle of the room adjusting her g-string. When she saw me her face split into a wide smile. In the more normal lighting of the dressing-room she looked even younger, about fourteen, and much prettier.

'Hi,' she said. 'I'm Francoise.'

'Hi,' I said.

'I have to go on in a minute, can you wait?'

'Sure.'

She glanced over her shoulder. The blonde girl was sitting at a table fronted by a large mirror, real backstage show-biz style. 'Remember,' Francoise said to the blonde, 'I saw him first.'

She squeezed tightly against me as she passed although there was no need, grinned up at me and hurried along the passageway her naked buttocks twitching invitingly as she went.

I turned back and caught the blonde girl looking at me through the mirror. There was a tiny frown cutting the otherwise smooth skin between her eyes.

'Hello, Linda,' I said.

The frown deepened and she spun round to stare directly at me. She was completely naked, not even the g-string she'd worn before covered her soft-skinned body. Unaccountably, I was embarrassed and looked away, settling for seeing her in the mirror. That way all I saw was her face and upper body. That was bad enough but it was better.

'My name's Bettina.'

'No it isn't. It's Linda Martin from Liverpool and your Dad's worried about you.'

'Who are you?'

'Mace.'

The frown faded. 'I thought I recognised you. I've seen your picture in the papers.'

'We met a few times as well,' I reminded her. 'But the last time you were only six.'

'You're a policeman.' The frown was back. 'Are you going to arrest me?'

'Why, what've you done?'

'Nothing. I mean, well, I suppose I am breaking the law just by working here.'

'No permit?'

She shook her head.

'Naughty. No, I'm over here on holiday and your Dad asked me to spend a little time looking for you. He's worried. Very worried.'

Her head drooped. 'I'm sorry. I suppose I should have called him but as time went on it got harder to know what to say.'

'Well, suppose you call him now, then I can begin enjoying myself.'

She reached out to pick up a tiny gold wristwatch. 'Not now, we have another gig.' Standing up she began to dress. Her lack of self-consciousness was disturbing.

She wasn't yet seventeen; how many other men had she stood before without clothes?

'Another gig?'

'A party in Hollywood, we're the cabaret, Ella and me.'

'Ella?'

She laughed. 'Francoise. Francoise and Bettina sounds better than Ella and Linda, doesn't it?'

Better for what, I thought. 'What time will you be through?' I asked.

'Two, three, something like that but we might be asked to stop.' She smiled brightly. 'Terry's parties are pretty exciting. Lots of famous people.'

'It only takes a few minutes to make a telephone call, even to England.'

She was almost fully dressed now; the reverse strip-tease hadn't helped my ambivalent state of mind. 'Tell you what,' she said. 'Come around to the house in the morning and we'll talk then.' She scribbled something on a scrap of paper. 'That's where we live, Ella and me.' She grinned cheekily. 'Ella will be very pleased to see you.'

I thought about arguing but there wasn't much point. I tried unsuccessfully to work out what time it was in England and came to the conclusion that whenever she called her father he would be happy about it. 'Okay,' I said. 'What time tomorrow?'

'Not too early, we'll be late home. Eleven?'

'Eleven,' I agreed.

The Mexican girl came back into the tiny dressing-room and smiled at me. It wasn't a come-on smile, just friendly. I smiled back. She glanced along the passage to where the fat man had dragged himself up into a crouch. I could hear a faint groaning over the sound of the music. 'Did you do that?' she asked.

'Sort of.'

'Time someone put him in his place, thanks.

I wasn't sure why she was thanking me but hazarded a guess that Fat Man was free with his hands.

Linda handed me the scrap of paper with her address, I read it and slipped it into my pocket. 'Eleven o'clock,' I said.

'Right.' She was close to me and I could tell she wanted to say something more. I waited. 'Back home, that time they wrote about you, put you on TV and everything. Dad didn't like it but I thought it was smashing.'

She meant the time I'd had a run-in with some villains after a bank job. I'd had to kill two and wound the third. I knew that Linda was complimenting me but it wasn't something I welcomed. Killing people isn't my idea of how a policeman does his job; especially when he's head of CID. I managed a smile for Linda. 'I'll see you tomorrow,' I said and went out.

As I clambered over Fat Man Ella-called-Francoise appeared at the end of the passageway.

'You're not going?' she said.

It crossed my mind that Linda might have been lying. 'Haven't you somewhere to go?'

She sighed theatrically. 'Terry's party. Another time?'

'Tomorrow.'

'Really?'

'Really. Ask Linda.'

I pushed past her, guiltily enjoying the feel of her naked breasts brushing against my chest. I wondered if somewhere in the United States there was another parent waiting hopefully for a telephone call from a straying daughter.

In the barroom it was silent. The disco music was

gone and so were the customers. It was seven o'clock in the evening. The stone-faced bartender was washing glasses.

'Closing?' I asked.

'It's the happy hour,' he said. 'Everybody goes to the joints that serve two drinks for the price of one.' He blew a mouthful of germs into a glass and polished them vigorously. 'They'll be back, the ones who like tits with their booze. Find what you wanted?'

I nodded and went across to lay Fat Man's gun and ammunition on the bar.

'If you ever come back,' the bartender advised, 'you better bring a coupla hand grenades and be ready to use them. He won't stop to ask if it was all a big mistake.'

'Thanks.'

'Don't thank me. I don't give a damn one way or the other but it's me that gets to mop up the blood.'

I grinned at him and went out into the bright evening.

My rental car was parked in a side street alongside the bar which stood on the junction of Coliseum and Rodeo. I drove east and joined the freeway system heading north, first on Harbor, passing the faintly seedy Downtown area with its convention centres and rising spires dedicated to making megabucks every second that ticked and casting into deeper shadows the skid-row district around 5th Street, then Hollywood which swept me along with more lanes in each direction than a pair of British motorways can manage all put together. I whisked past Paramount studios, the Hollywood Bowl and Universal City, finally taking Ventura going west. Here it wasn't as classy as it hoped it was but the final bright rays of the setting sun helped hide the odd example of tinselled tawdriness that spoiled the prevailing image.

It wasn't a good way to see the city, just a means of

seeing a few thousand motor cars all surprisingly observing a speed limit that would have had any self-respecting East Lancs cowboy in fits of frustration.

I had a room at Steele's Motor Lodge on Ventura Boulevard so I dropped off the freeway at Coldwater, reflecting that I'd just driven enough miles to get me from the police station where I worked in east Liverpool to the airport in Manchester from where I'd caught the flight to LA. And I hadn't covered a fraction of the distance needed to get me out of this sprawling city. Most places I visit I reckon the local law has some things easy; here, so far as logistics was concerned, I wasn't so sure.

At the motel I showered and shaved, then changed my clothes for something snappier than I'd chosen to go bar-crawling. I'd switched on the TV out of a reflex born of not liking rooms that were filled only with the sound of my own breathing. A news broadcast was following the departure from LA of the American vice-president. He'd been here to boost the election chances of a tall, rangy, young-looking man with prematurely white hair and the manner of a European aristocrat who was running for governor.

If the reporter was anything to go by, voting would be a formality. The news item changed to one about earth-tremors in San Diego so I turned the set off and went out, having already decided to eat at The Tail of the Cock which was a couple of miles or so east on Ventura. The attraction for me was the house pianist. Johnny Guarnieri once played with Benny Goodman and as a small boy had been a protégé of Fats Waller.

He was playing at a piano-bar, one of those things I thought only existed in the minds of Hollywood set designers. The piano has a bar built all around it, with seats facing inwards. You couldn't get any closer to the musical action without sitting in the piano-player's lap.

Guarnieri was playing softly; house rules, I guessed. Mustn't let the music drown the vapid, self-centred chatter of the people who were there to be seen and heard, not to listen to a piano-player however good he was. And he *was* good.

I eventually tore myself away to follow a waiter to a table where I ate a steak that elsewhere would have tasted only so-so. Thanks to the music it tasted a hundred times better than any steak I'd ever eaten.

When I came out it was past ten and the car hop scurried away to find my car. He'd hidden it well out of sight. A Chevette doesn't rate alongside a string of a dozen or two Rolls-Royces and Mercedes.

As I waited a retinue of black limousines slid into the parking lot and drew up by the entrance to the restaurant. A half dozen or so men scrambled out. They all had the hard, professional look of paid assassins, so had to be bodyguards in this environment. When they were sure no bomb-throwers lurked in the shadows a man climbed leisurely out of the biggest of the cars. I recognised him instantly from the TV newscast. I was within arm's reach of the leading candidate for state governor. If the heavy mob was anything to go by some people thought he was important, or maybe just he did.

Under the white hair an unlined, tanned face looked my way. He was older than me by a good ten years but he looked as if he could have run me into the ground. Amazing what orange juice, jogging, perpetual sunshine and a few early nights can do for the complexion. He smiled, displaying perfect white teeth. The smile was wasted, I didn't have a vote.

I drove back along Ventura, right into Van Nuys and pulled into the filling station on the corner. I asked the attendant for directions to Carmelo's and he told me that if I fell out of my car I would crack my head on its sidewall.

That seemed a little extreme but he looked as though he'd had a hard day. I parked the Chevette in the alley behind the club, then walked around to the front entrance; it was a still, warm night, the kind Liverpool gets about once every two hundred years. I wasn't the slightest bit homesick.

Carmelo's is the leading jazz club in Los Angeles and when I'd called the LA Jazzline the recorded message had assured me that Monday night was big band night and tonight it was the turn of the Bill Berry LA Band. I'd met Bill once when he played a town north of Liverpool with the Louis Bellson Explosion and then again when he toured England as a solo. I was curious to know how he sounded with his own band and on his own turf. Terrific, was the answer.

I stood at the back of the room, drinking Michelob out of the bottle and beginning to relax for the first time in years.

The room at Carmelo's isn't large, maybe fifty feet long and twenty wide. With a sixteen-piece band blowing their collective buns off down at one end it was positively intimate. The tables are arranged with seats at one side so no one need have his back to the bandstand. The bar runs down most of the left-hand side and was two-deep with the more serious drinkers.

Visibility wasn't good, cigarette smoke accounted for a real LA smog and the lighting was turned way down. I was growing accustomed to the local natives' disaffection for bright lights in their watering-holes; anyway, here it suited.

My interest in music went back to the cradle. My father was a semi-pro saxophone-player who worked the Liverpool dance halls from long before I was born right up to the sixties. That was when the Beatles had changed the face of the city's music forever.

He'd packed it in then, concentrating on his full-time job on the docks for the last couple of years until retirement brought vegetation and a quick death.

He'd never said so, but I know he regretted that although I'd always been interested in music I'd never taken the trouble to learn an instrument. I regretted it too, especially when I heard what I was hearing now.

I was at the bar, buying my third bottle of beer when I saw a face I recognised among the paying customers. I'd already seen a dozen faces I knew from record sleeves up on the bandstand but this was a more recent and a decidedly non-musical acquaintance.

At the far end of the bar, where it turns in to the sidewall, is a small space with a few seats. The back wall is mirrored and standing there, watching and listening to the band, was the stone-faced bartender I'd seen earlier that evening at The Blue Whale, the joint where Linda did her dance. I was surprised to see him, although there was no reason why I should have been.

Almost an hour later Stoneface left his corner. Instinctively cautious, I buried my face in one hand secretively studying his pushed-in profile as he passed me. I couldn't tell if he was enjoying himself. Out of nothing more than idle curiosity I followed.

On the sidewalk a handful of people stood taking advantage of the fact that out here the music could still be heard and the oxygen level was noticeably higher.

Stoneface was walking south, towards the adjacent filling station. Before he reached it a black limousine slid into the curb and stopped. The bartender opened the door as if he was expecting to be picked up, climbed aboard and the car whispered off again.

Like most policemen I have a reflex action born of

long hours watching comings and goings of all kinds in all sorts of places; I registered the licence plate number.

Then I heard the band begin Ellington's 'Rockin' in Rhythm' and went back inside.

It was two o'clock before the band ended its final set and I took the opportunity of reminding Bill Berry where we'd met and what my name was. Surprisingly, he remembered.

'You had a little girl with you,' he said. 'Your daughter.'

'That's right.'

'I remember because she seemed kind of young to be at a jazz concert.'

'She was six then, at that age she didn't carry enough weight to argue. It was my weekend to have her and I didn't want to miss the show.'

'Is she with you now?'

I shook my head. My wife had remarried a couple of years ago and it seemed better to let our daughter settle for one father instead of two. He wasn't a bad guy, which is to say he didn't have any form. I'd checked. It floated across my mind that she was eleven next month. Five more years and she would be as old as Linda was when she left home, six years and she'd be the age Linda is now. Who'd be a father?

Something in my face must have shown I didn't want to talk about my family anymore. Apart from being nice people jazz musicians are sensitive. Comes with the job, I suppose. Policemen are sensitive too, but have less opportunity to be nice.

Bill and I talked some more and then it was time to go so I went out the backway with the band, was introduced to most of them and said farewell almost in the same breath and then drove the short distance to the motel.

Not surprisingly I overslept next morning. I quickly

put on light blue slacks and a white cotton jacket which would have earned curious looks in Liverpool and headed for Linda's, making better time than I'd expected and aware that lack of sleep or not, I was hungry.

Along the way I ate breakfast. Not the superhuman meal most Americans seem able to feed themselves on but toast and coffee. I'll do most things as the Romans do, but I like my eating habits to remain constant.

Burlington Avenue was a small, shabby street just off MacArthur Park. The whole district looked rundown and was litter-strewn. It didn't look like something to write a song about but then the same could be said for most of Liverpool. That hadn't stopped Lennon and McCartney.

The house was a small, stucco-walled single-storey building with a blue pantiled roof. The front wall of the house was painted pink, the sidewalls white. All the paint was peeling. For some reason peeling pink looked worse than peeling white.

Although it wasn't yet eleven o'clock the heat was oppressive, beating down on me as though I'd done the sun an injustice. A dog and a cat were lying a few yards apart near where I parked. The dog had one eye open, its muzzle flat to the ground. The cat had both eyes closed. It knew it was too hot for the dog to chase it.

Across the street a radio was playing 1930s dance music. It could've been Buddy Rogers or Richard Himber or any one of those bland soundalike bands.

I stood in the hot sun trying not to sweat and pressed the doorbell, listening to it echoing inside. After the bell stopped I could hear a faint buzzing sound. It might have been cicadas but sounded too regular. No one came to the door. I tried not to breathe in case I seared my lungs. On balance I preferred last night's smoke.

After a while I walked around the left side of the house. Through a half-curtained window I could see a sparsely-furnished slightly untidy living-room which ran the full length of the house. Around the back was a small patch of dusty garden. The back door opened into a kitchen. I tried the door; it too was locked. Coming back up the other side of the house I passed an obscured-glass window I took to be the bathroom, then a window which revealed a neat and tidy bedroom with no one in it. The buzzing was louder now and when I reached the next window it was obviously coming from there. The blind was down and I could see nothing. That brought me back to the front door again where I tried the bell once more.

The street still slumbered in the heat. Nothing moved. Even the dog had given up and closed its other eye. The radio station was still playing dance music and a woman in a thin, approximate soprano was trying to join in. After a couple of choruses, she gave up the unequal struggle.

I went quickly around the house to the back door. A few bits of metal and wood were lying in the dirt. I found something that could have been a part of an old lawnmower and used it to commit an illegal act on the door. It made more noise than I would have liked but no one paid any attention.

The kitchen was a mess. Whoever kept house here, didn't. From the smell most of the cooking seemed to have been well-laced with peppers and garlic. Unwashed dishes were piled in the sink and there were enough open and empty cans to fill a truck.

A telephone was fixed to one wall alongside a piece of blackboard on which were scrawled telephone numbers, half a recipe for chili con carne and a not-bad drawing of Fritz the Cat. A balloon coming out of his mouth said something obscene, but then, Fritz usually does.

I checked the bathroom. Talk about stockings in the basin when a feller wants a shave! There was enough assorted feminine underwear around to keep a knicker-fetishist in orgasm for a year. The mirror was cracked and the bath had rust-stains beneath both taps.

Across the narrow passage was a door into the long living-room. I'd already seen through the window that no one was in there but I looked anyway. It had a dusty, unlived-in smell. A TV set had a drooping indoor aerial perched on top of it and an old-fashioned cabinet radiogram was piled high with records, otherwise it looked as homely as a bus-station waiting room.

Next was the neat bedroom. A photograph in a cheap wooden frame stood on a table by the bed. The picture was of Linda, her father and her mother who had died a couple of years back. Linda wore a school uniform. Two years on and she wore a g-string to work. I'd seen the picture before; a smaller version of it was in my wallet. That was all I'd had for identification. The bed hadn't been slept in.

The next door led me into the room with the drawn blind but even so it was light enough to see clearly. The mess in here made the kitchen look like something from a palace. Clothes everywhere, dropped where their owner had stepped out of them. Unless . . .

A bedsheet lay across someone lying still on the bed. Only the feet were visible. The toenails were painted purple.

I reached out a cautious hand and rested the back of it against one foot. It was cold. I clasped my fingers around the ankle, feeling for a pulse. Nothing.

Carefully, I pulled the sheet back from the head. The

face was a little different to when I had last seen Ella-called-Francoise. For one thing dead eyes replaced those that had danced brightly and suggestively at me. Alongside the right eye was a large contusion. The nose was bruised and a thin trickle of blood had run from one nostril to dry on her top lip. More blood had run from her mouth, mingling with something else that had dried yellow. Vomit, maybe, I couldn't tell.

I pulled the sheet back a little more until I could see her neck. The marks were blue-black and yellowish-green. Manual strangulation. Surprisingly enough, I hadn't seen one before. Strangulations, yes, but they'd all been done with some help: a tie, a scarf, a belt, a length of wire.

I let the sheet fall back across Ella's face which, despite the injuries and death-pallor, now looked like a twelve-year old's and stood for a moment, thinking. Then I stretched across the bed to turn off the buzzing alarm clock. Automatically I checked the time it was set for. Eleven o'clock. It was now a quarter past.

I knew all the rules, of course. Maybe not the American rules word for word but they couldn't be very much different from those I worked to back home. But I broke them all the same.

It didn't do any good. I could only risk a swift search; first Ella's room, then Linda's, then the large living room. Maybe a detailed search would turn up something of interest but I couldn't take a chance on disturbing too much.

I went back into the kitchen and picked the telephone off the hook with finger and thumb carefully placed near the earphone end. I used a ballpoint pen to dial. It felt strange, calling the police.

In the past I'd often met people who had failed to

report discovering bodies immediately, if at all. They'd all said they were afraid even though they'd done nothing wrong. For the first time I understood. I wasn't afraid, but I did have an uneasy feeling that I was involved in something that wouldn't go away quite as quickly as it had come.

Chapter Two

The prowl car arrived exactly three minutes after I'd put down the phone. Pretty good going. By then I was out on the street leaning against my simmering rental car and listening to the radio in the house across the way. The music had hotted up and Lionel Hampton was rattling through 'Central Avenue Breakdown.'

The patrolmen were young, tall and tough. I was older but not much, taller by even less but I wasn't too sure about being tougher. One of them looked as if he ate fencing posts for lunch. In most respects they could have been twins: hatless, their neatly-cut hair was clean and blond above round, tanned faced. Their eyes were hidden behind regulation-issue sunglasses and their uniforms were crisp models of sartorial elegance. Not the thing for a Saturday afternoon's crowd control at Anfield. They wore name tags on their shirts to assist public relations, or to make complaints easier to personalise.

I explained enough to interest them and we all went inside through the back door. I showed them Ella's body. Then we all trooped into the kitchen where the fence-post eater whose name tag identified him as J. G. Mullany started asking questions. From the tone he used and the way his questions were slanted it was clear he thought it was an open-and-shut case. I'd done it.

His partner cooled the atmosphere a little by asking politely for some identification. I slowly took my wallet out. Mullany twitched as my hand went inside my jacket. I slipped the money out of the wallet, and pocketed it thus leaving Mullany's partner free to make a search without being compromised.

'You know the girl,' Mullany said.

It wasn't exactly a question. 'Her name is Ella, I don't know her last name,' I told him. 'Look, don't you think we should wait for homicide?'

His eyebrows clamped down over the bar across the top of his sunglasses. 'What the hell do you know. You're not even American. What the hell kind of accent is that anyway?'

'English,' I said politely.

'So keep your nose clean,' he said which didn't seem to fit but I shrugged and waited.

His partner's name was Carling and I could see he'd finally got to my warrant card and was reading it as if he'd never seen one before. I don't suppose he had, not exactly. He looked at me curiously over the top of his dark glasses.

'What were you doing here, anyway?' Mullany wanted to know.

'I was calling on another girl who lives here.'

'Why?'

'I'm a friend of her father's.'

'Shit! Is that the best you can do?'

I heard a car door slam out in the street and Mullany heard it too. He turned on his heel and marched out of the kitchen and up the passageway towards the front door.

'Is he always like that or is it something in my face?' I asked Carling.

'He can't help it, he's from Philadelphia and hasn't had time to acclimatise.' He handed me my wallet. 'Detective Chief Superintendent. Sounds impressive. What's that equivalent to?'

I thought for a moment. 'Somewhere around Captain of Detectives I think.'

He whistled softly. 'Just wait until Bercovici hears that.'

'Bercovici?'

'Lieutenant Bercovici, Homicide. That's Bercovici out there now.' He jerked a thumb towards the front of the house. 'The lieutenant hates all senior ranks.' He was still going through my wallet, passing incuriously over the picture of Linda and her parents.

Mullany appeared at the kitchen door. 'The lieutenant wants you,' he said to Carling.

Carling handed me back my wallet.

Mullany came over and put his bar-bending eyebrows an inch from mine. 'Try leaving and I will personally blow your ass off,' he promised.

'Why would I leave? I like the company.'

He glowered, obviously trying to think of some legitimate reason for shooting me on the spot. Failing to come up with one he turned away and stomped after his partner.

I rummaged around the untidy work surfaces of the kitchen until I found a fairly clean pan. I half-filled it with water, then put it on the stove to boil. Coffee was harder to find but I eventually tracked some down at the back of a cupboard. I hoped Lieutenant Bercovici wouldn't hate me for putting my fingerprints all over the kitchen but I didn't think it would do much harm. When the water boiled I made instant coffee in a beaker I had to wash first. The sludge at the bottom of a milk bottle had turned itself into something approaching cheese so I took the coffee black.

For want of something to do I stood reading the

telephone numbers on the blackboard by the phone. One number was written alongside the name 'Terry'. I remembered that was the name Linda had mentioned when she's talked about the party she and Ella were going to.

I scribbled the number down on a dollar bill, then replaced all my money in my wallet.

For a fleeting moment I was tempted to erase the number from the blackboard. I had a feeling Terry was bad news and I wanted to protect Linda's reputation, but I did nothing.

'Detective Chief Superintendent Mace?' a voice enquired. It was a woman's voice, husky and quiet.

I turned to see her standing in the doorway. She was tall, almost as tall as me although her three-inch heels helped. She was wearing an oatmeal-coloured skirt that came halfway down calves which appeared flawless in both design and construction. She wore a dark-brown shirt, open lower than was advisable among hot-blooded males and over it a lightweight cotton coat that mixed both colours in irregular stripes. Her hair was long and brown with a hint of chestnut. Her eyes were also brown, very dark, fringed with extra long lashes and surrounded with delicately applied green make-up. She was sensational.

'Yes,' I said. 'But you can call me sweetheart.'

She didn't smile. She didn't look as if she smiled very often. 'My name is Bercovici,' she said. 'But you can call me Lieutenant.'

I have nothing against policewomen. I've worked with good ones and indifferent ones. Rarely though, in plain clothes work, have I seen one above the rank of inspector. Maybe that was roughly equivalent to lieutenant but I had a feeling, reinforced by countless American TV cop shows I'd seen, that police lieutenants out here did rather more top-line detecting than our inspectors do back home. Especially on murder cases. But then, out here they have more murders than us. A whole lot more.

'Tell me what you know,' she said.

I did as she asked. I missed out the bit about kicking the fat man in the stomach because I didn't want her to think I made a habit of such things. Nor did I tell her about seeing the bartender from The Blue Whale in Carmelo's or that I'd seen him climb into a car the number of which I'd memorised. There was no reason why I should.

I did tell her about the party at Terry's but left if to her to find the number on the blackboard. After all, it could be another Terry.

About Linda I held nothing back. Mainly because I wanted to find the girl as soon as possible and I guessed Lieutenant Bercovici would too. On that score we were both on the same side. Anyway, by now I guessed that Officer Carling would have seen the picture in Linda's bedroom and would remember it from my wallet.

'You're in California as a private citizen,' she said when I was through.

'Yes.'

'No official standing of any kind?'

'None at all. Just on holiday, vacation. And doing a favour for an old friend.'

'Where are you living?'

I gave her the address and phone number of the motel.

'How long will you be in town?'

'Until Linda turns up and calls home to her father. Then I'm heading north to San Francisco.'

'There's no reason to stay around, Chief Superintendent. If you call in periodically, we'll let you know when we've found the girl.'

I smiled politely. 'I feel, well, responsible.'

'Responsible?'

'Her father and I are good friends.'

I'd known Ken Martin since schooldays. I was a popular kid, not because of any personal qualities but because my mother worked part-time in the local flea-pit. The 1950s were still picturegoing days in Liverpool, like most places in England. Bingo and TV had a grip but it wasn't yet a stranglehold.

My mother let me in the front door almost every night, in turn I let my mates in the side door. For a consideration, of course. In Ken Martin's case I made no charge because *his* mother worked in the city's biggest record store which was where we spent our Saturday mornings, and afternoons too when the lads were playing away.

The fact that Ken had become a solicitor, often defending the villains I brought to court, hadn't disturbed a friendship forged in such a mutually beneficial manner.

Ken had gone through a bad patch when his wife was killed in a car smash. I'd helped all I could, which I don't suppose was much. My ex-wife had helped even more because she'd been close to Linda's mother. In fact it was a period when it looked as if we might get together again but good sense prevailed on both sides. There are some things it isn't smart to do; going back to a place where you were happy once is another of them.

The beautiful lieutenant was studying me curiously.

'If it's all the same to you, I'll stick around until I know Linda's safe,' I said.

'And if it isn't all the same to me?' she asked.

'I'll stick around anyway. Unless you want to throw me in gaol. I'm sure Officer Mullany will be happy to help out if you can't manage it yourself.'

Her eyes hardened. 'One thing you should learn

from the start, Mace. I don't need help from any man, especially Officer Mullany and most especially of all, you.'

She turned and stalked back along the passageway towards a flock of men coming in through the front door. I recognised the gear they were carrying. Curious to see how their murder squads operated I wandered along to Ella's bedroom and watched. Everything seemed to be happening the way it did back home, so I went outside and stood in the sparse shade of an ailing pepper tree.

Across the street the radio station had done an about turn and was bleating out some Twenties Whiteman. The cracked soprano was giving it another whirl. The tune was 'Dardanella' and not only was she off-key but she also sang straight across Bix's solo. Some people have no taste.

I heard feet shuffle in the dust and saw Officer Mullany was guarding the front door. He chose to ignore me. I guessed he had heard I was just one of the boys.

Half an hour passed before Lieutenant Bercovici came out and I was only mildly fried. If it hadn't been for the tree I would've melted.

'Anything?' I asked.

'It has nothing to do with you,' she said.

I saw a big nasty grin on Mullany's face and stepped closer to the lady and lowered my voice. 'Look, I'm here and I'm staying. Now maybe I haven't your charm and good looks but I'm not an amateur. I didn't make Detective Chief Superintendent by brown-nosing. I made it because I'm a good copper.'

'This is America, not England.'

'Good coppery is good coppery, anywhere in the world.'

She thought about this for a moment, then something which could have been a smile floated across the back of her eyes. 'Can you take orders or are you too set on being the boss?'

'I can take orders.' I grinned. 'If they're the right ones.'

She almost smiled but managed not to. 'Okay, you can stay around but don't get in the way. Meet me at the precinct house tomorrow morning, nine o'clock.'

'Tomorrow morning? It's only midday.'

She looked at me pityingly. 'In case you hadn't heard we have a higher crime rate over here. Not as bad as New York or Philadelphia but bad enough, certainly a whole lot worse than you have back home in little old London town.'

'Liverpool,' I reminded her.

'Even more to the point. I don't have the luxury of working on one case at a time, Mace. I have five at the moment, a rape, an aggravated assault, an armed robbery in which two people were shot and wounded and one other homicide. Between now and nine o'clock tomorrow I hope to have at least two of those cases off my list in order to make space for the two or three more that will come in during that same period of time. Anyway, between now and then, maybe Linda will turn up without any help from us.'

I know when I'm licked. 'Nine o'clock,' I said.

'Right.'

I watched as she walked smartly across the street to her car. In climbing in her skirt rode up and her thighs looked as good as her calves. She saw me looking and took off faster than was necessary. I turned to see Mullany had also been studying anatomy. Our eyes met and he scowled. I don't think he was convinced I wasn't the strangler, warrant card or no warrant card.

I drove back to the motel where I lay on the bed in my room cooling off and thinking about the next move. The bartender and the black limo were probably a blind alley and even if they weren't I didn't know how to trace a licence number in this town. The telephone number belonging to someone named Terry who might or might not be the same Terry the girls were visiting last night wasn't much easier.

I reached for the phone and dialled the number. No one answered so I gave that up and went back to thinking. I still had the fat man, who would probably kill me sooner than talk to me, and the Mexican girl.

I went out and drove across town to The Blue Whale. It was three o'clock when I walked inside and the contrast between the burning sun in the street and the cool gloom of the interior was almost physical.

There was no sign of Fat Man but I played it safe and didn't turn my back on any dark corners or doorways.

The bartender was in place and the music was as loud as ever. Custom was better today, maybe a dozen deadbeats lined the bar. The Mexican girl was dancing. She wasn't working her way along, just standing there pulsating to the music. I guessed she was under orders to take her time until they replaced Ella. And Linda? It wasn't a happy thought.

The naked girl recognised me and smiled. The bartender also recognised me. He didn't smile. He came out from behind the bar, jerked his head and went through the doorway. I followed cautiously but Fat Man wasn't lying in wait.

'Where the hell are they?' the bartender demanded.

'Who?'

'Francoise and Bettina, for Chrissake, who do you think I mean?'

'How should I know?'

He sighed. 'Look, mister, I've no beef one way or the other. For all I care you can be a white-slaver and you can dance on Roccisano's guts any time you like but I need my girls. You don't think those bums out there use my bar because they like looking at *my* face do you?'

It was probably the longest speech he'd ever made in his life. He really was wound up. At least I had the fat man's name without having to ask for it.

'Where is Roccisano?' I asked.

'Uptown someplace. On business.'

'What does he do here?'

His eyes looked cagey, like he'd just stepped into the ring with a man two weights up and ten years younger. 'He uses the office, that's all. Nothing illegal.'

'Would I care if it was?'

'Cops always care about things like that.'

I thought about denying I was a policeman but decided not to bother. 'You own this place?' I asked instead.

'Me? You're kidding. I run the joint. The owner sits up in the hills where it's cool in the summer and in the winter he goes to the Bahamas anyway.'

We were becoming old buddies. 'The owner know about Roccisano?'

'What does he care?' He grinned suddenly. 'Sure is madder'n hell with you. Nobody's taken a gun off of him since he was eight years old.'

'I bet.' I looked at him for a moment. 'Both girls leave soon after me yesterday?' I asked.

'Yeah, they had a job in Coldwater Canyon.'

'Oh? Another bar?'

He laughed. 'In Coldwater Canyon? You're kidding.'

'Where then?'

His face closed up, back to old Stoneface. 'What's it to you?'

'Could be less trouble to tell me.'

'What's happened to those girls?'

'Why should anything have happened?'

'Because they're missing and you're here asking questions. Maybe you don't dress like one and you sure as hell don't speak like one, but you smell like one.'

'Like what?'

'Cop.'

I took out my wallet and flicked the edges of some bills. 'Private and generous,' I told him.

He shook his head. 'Can't help you and even if I could, Roccisano isn't a man to cross as you'll find out if he catches up with you.'

'What time did you leave here last night?'

'What's it to you?'

I took hold of a large piece of his shirt front. 'I could ask you another way.'

'I was here until we closed, then I went home.'

'What time was that?'

'The same time as every night. Around one.'

It didn't sound like a lie and if I hadn't known it to be one I would have been fooled. 'And where's home?' I enquired.

'Across the street.'

I let him go. 'I want to talk to the girl,' I said. 'The Mexican girl on the bar right now.'

'For Chrissake, I only got the two left out of five.'

'So put the other one on and send the Mexican out here.'

He shook his head then went down the passage. He banged on the door at the far end and it opened and a tiny, birdlike black girl came out. The two argued for a few seconds but she gave up easily. They both went through the door halfway along the passage and maybe a minute later the Mexican girl came through the door to where I waited.

'Where are Linda and Ella?' she asked.

At least she knew their real names. 'In trouble,' I said. 'Very bad trouble. The cops will be around here in the morning asking a lot of very tough questions. It might help to talk to me now.'

'What do you want to know?'

'Any special friends they had, anything they've been into they shouldn't have been.'

She shrugged. 'Lots of friends, all men. We all have. You don't think this job pays us enough to live.'

An image of Linda, fresh out of school, floated across my mind's eye I thrust it away. 'Names?'

'Harry, Joe, Sonny, Mac, Richie, Jerry . . .'

'No last names?' I interrupted.

'Men don't have last names,' she said.

'How about Terry?'

She frowned. 'From the studio?'

'That's the one, lives up in Coldwater Canyon,' I guessed.

'That's where Linda and Ella went last night to do their act.'

'So what's his last name?'

'Terry's not a man. She's Terita Montez. She makes movies.'

'Oh?'

'You know, pornos.'

'Oh.'

She laughed suddenly. 'You're shocked.'

I nodded my head. 'I haven't seen Linda since she was six years old. She only left school a year ago. It takes some adjusting to.'

She was as suddenly solemn. 'I'm sorry, I shouldn't have laughed.'

'Do you know this Terry's address?'

'Not her home, just that she lives off Coldwater. The studio is on Van Nuys way up near the top. I went there a couple of times.' She shrugged. 'It pays well.'

'This act that Linda and Ella did, what was it exactly?'

'The usual. You know the kind of thing two girls do together.'

I did. 'They were doing it last night at a party?'

'Sure, pays even better than the movies.'

'Thanks . . . what's your name?'

'Lorelei,' she said.

'Your real name.'

She grinned. 'Maria, what else?'

'Thanks, Maria.'

'Is it bad?'

I didn't want to screw up Lieutenant Bercovici's interrogation tomorrow but I liked this girl. 'Very bad,' I told her. 'Be careful what you do and who you do it with.'

'Don't worry, I'll be out of town before your feet hit the street.'

'The police will want to talk to you tomorrow.'

'You bet they will, especially when they know I'm here without papers.'

'Oh.'

'So I'll just take a trip south of the border until the dust settles.'

'Take care of yourself,' I told her.

'No, you take care of yourself,' she said. 'The trouble is where you're headed.'

She was right, I thought, as I went out into the street. I had a porno movie maker who also put on live shows, with a studio in Van Nuys and a home in Coldwater Canyon. I also had a lying bartender who told me he'd been around here all night when I'd seen him, apparently all innocent, in a jazz club that was also on Van Nuys.

I didn't know what it all added up to but there wasn't much doubt that I was in the wrong part of town.

I headed northwest, stopping along the way at a post office to look at a telephone directory.

I had no idea what hours porno movie makers kept but as all I had was Terita Montez's home address that was where I went.

The telephone book had told me she lived in Vedado Avenue off Coldwater Canyon Avenue. Vedado is a winding tree-lined street among a lot of other winding tree-lined streets. The many houses stand discreetly and securely back from the roadway, all well-hidden among thick trees many of them flowering and sending delicate perfumes into the hot air. The Montez house also had a high wall around it with double wrought-iron gates being the only way through short of commando tactics or a bulldozer. I settled for ringing the bell.

A voice squawked at me from a grille set into the wall. I told the grille my name was Mace because there didn't seem any point in lying about it and that I was a friend of Francoise and Bettina's and that Roccisano was my bosom-buddy.

There was a long silence during which I listened to the cicadas, thinking about the alarm-clock buzzing unavailingly beside Ella's bedside.

Then something went 'clunk' and the gates opened all by themselves. I climbed back into the car, thinking wasn't science wonderful, and drove through.

The drive was short and lined with a low wall on one side and a high hedge on the other. The wall spilled over with purple and red bougainvillaea while the hedge tried to match its splendour with brilliant yellow star-shaped flowers.

The house was a cross between the Starship Enterprise and Frank Lloyd Wright copy. Fourth carbon. I stopped in front of what I guessed was the main entrance although it could have been an opening into another galaxy judging by all the bits of coloured glass and electronic gadgetry.

The door opened as I climbed out of the car. I thought at first this was another piece of scientific wizardry but then I saw the door had been opened by a midget. She was about three feet high and dressed as what looked for all the world like a colour-blind, middle-aged Shirley Temple.

She stared at me questioningly.

'Terita Montez?'

She went off into a high-pitched peal of near-hysterical laughter and walked back into the house leaving the door open.

I assumed I was supposed to follow her, so I did. She went right on through the house and out into the garden beyond. It was a spacious house, or at least the parts I saw were. A main room about thirty feet square was furnished in early-kitsch, all lace and frills and twee ornaments in colours that made the midget's frock look suitable for Sunday School. One thing noticeable was that despite the lack of taste that had gone into the décor, the room was immaculate: no cigarette ends in the ash-trays, no canapes ground into the carpet, no damp rings on the polished surfaces and the air was faintly scented with what could have been hibiscus. If there'd been a party here last night it wasn't in this room.

Ceiling-high glass doors opened into the garden which was where the midget had gone. There was a swimming-pool, sunlight glinting on its rippled turquoise water, a poolside bar that looked like a prop for a Hawaiian holiday brochure, various bits of uncomfortable-looking steel and plastic furniture and a view that was worth flying six thousand miles for. Most of Los Angeles was spread out below and it was almost possible to forgive the interior decorator who had ravished the house and the architect whose imagination had fallen short of his ambition.

The midget seemed to have disappeared but someone was rising from the pool, dripping water and irritation. She was medium height, about forty-five I would guess, and too thin for my taste. A minute one-piece bright yellow bathing suit was pasted on her front with holes cut just about everywhere. She had the kind of neck that gets left on the plate after a Thanksgiving dinner.

'So you're Mace,' she said, still towelling her dark hair.

'Terita Montez, I hope.'

She laughed. Now I could see that her face was sharp, like a thin alley-cat. A small nose was set between eyes that could have been black. Despite the lack of cover for her body her skin was untanned and apart from her wrinkled neck and matching elbows she was in good shape for a woman of her age.

'Clara told me you mistook her for me.' She glanced around and I saw the midget come out from behind the Hawaiian bar with a tray on which she balanced a large jug of orange juice, a bottle of what turned out to be vodka and three long glasses.

'Sit down, Mr Mace,' Terita Montez said, 'and tell me what you want.'

I did as I was told and the midget fussed around pouring drinks for the three of us. 'Two girls were here last night at your party. Francoise and Bettina, real names Ella and Linda. I'm looking for them.'

‘A party? Here?’ She glanced at Clara. ‘I don’t remember a party here last night, do you?’

Clara laughed again, just as loud and hysterical as before.

‘Do you know these girls?’ I asked.

‘I know a lot of people. Do they have last names?’

‘Linda Martin, I don’t know Ella’s last name.’

‘No, I don’t think I can help you.’ She smiled insincerely at me. ‘What is your interest in them?’ The smile turned evil. ‘Like them at seventeen, do you?’

‘Is that how old they are?’ I enquired politely.

The smile faded. ‘You’re a cop. The accent threw me for a while but you’re a cop. No wonder . . .’ She broke off abruptly and buried her face in the glass of vodka and orange.

‘You make porno movies,’ I said.

‘So what? It isn’t illegal here, whatever it may be in your half-assed little country.’ Her voice had started out thin and harsh, now it was getting strident.

‘Look, Miss Montez, I really don’t care a damn for what you do, how you do it, or who you do it with. I would very much like to find Linda Martin. Soon and without any trouble. Can you help?’

She looked at me, running her eyes from somewhere around my chest up over my face and up to a point three feet over my head. She smiled again and this time it was with pleasure.

I came up out of the chair, awkward and ducking low. Something whistled past my ear and hit the back of the chair I’d just vacated.

It was Roccisano, the fat man. He was holding what looked like a piece of steel tubing and judging from the mess it had made of my chair that’s exactly what it was. The damage also told me that his intentions were fatal.

I dropped into a fighting crouch, weighing the odds.

Roccisano grinned and showed me his gun. I shouldn't have left it for him, back at The Blue Whale. He lumbered forward, steel pipe in one hand, gun in the other. Some people never learn.

I moved in fast, feet first and hit him hard in the stomach. This time I wasn't quite so lucky. The breath came out of his body with a great whoosh and he dropped the tubing. He didn't drop the gun.

I swept up the broken chair and hit him with it as he fired. The shot echoed loud in my ears but it was the only one he would loose off at me. The gun went flying through the air to land far enough away to do me no more harm. Roccisano steadied himself, then came at me in an elephantine rush. There was no room to dodge sideways, and to stand still or move towards him would have hurt me more than it would hurt him. So I went backwards, letting his enormous weight flounder helplessly against my unresisting body. I'd forgotten I was on the edge of a swimming-pool. We both went in.

In the water he was more agile than out. In the water his weight no longer counted for much. I grabbed hold of his head and pulled him under, then managed to get my foot under his chin.

I pushed down and simultaneously let myself rise up. My head broke surface and I took a breath. Roccisano's head was on the bottom, wedged there by my foot.

I could see Terita Montez and Clara standing by the pool looking towards us. I didn't have time to see what they thought of it all before Roccisano's hands grasped at me and pulled me downwards. I didn't mind, I had more air in my lungs than he had in his. I could wait.

He let go in a matter of seconds and I took another gulp of air. From the bottom of the pool a cloud of bubbles forced their way to the surface. I took my foot from the fat man's neck. I didn't want to kill him, even if he didn't feel the same way about me.

He lurched to the surface like a harpooned whale and I took a handful of his hair and swam for the side.

I heaved myself up and out and stayed on my knees by the poolside getting my breath back. I'd need it. Hauling the fat man out of the water was likely to prove a major undertaking.

I saw Clara coming towards me. She was carrying the jug of orange juice. I thought it was a strange time to be serving drinks. Then I realised she had other plans in mind. I tried to scramble up off my knees but the struggle in the pool had taken more out of me than I'd suspected. Her pudgy, physically retarded face was creased in a malevolent grin, then the jug she was swinging hit me on the side of the head. I heard more than felt the jug shatter with the force of the blow and I keeled over sideways and back into the pool.

When the waters of the pool closed over me they were no longer turquoise. Now they were black.

Chapter Three

Someone was dancing on my chest. I waved a feeble hand and the dancing stopped. Rolling over onto my side I spewed out a bathtubful of water. Opening my eyes I saw that it had gone into the swimming pool which seemed only right. Sitting up, I could see that the chest-dancer was Officer Carling. He was wet.

'Thanks,' I said. My mouth tasted of chlorine.

He grinned behind his sunglasses. 'Anytime.'

'I should thank you, Mr Mace,' a thin voice cut in. It was Terita Montez, all demure in a printed cotton dress with a high neck. I wondered what had happened to the yellow swimsuit. 'If it hadn't been for your bravery, heaven knows what that prowler might have done.'

While I was working out what she was talking about I noticed two things. One was that another lady was present. She was tiny and stooped, maybe about seventy with dry grey hair and a vaguely familiar look. The other thing I noticed was that there was no one in the swimming pool. I checked all around me. Roccisano had vanished.

Terita Montez hadn't finished. 'And if it hadn't been foı you hearing the gunshot, Miss Jerome, why, we'd all be dead.'

I took it that the little old lady was Miss Jerome.

'What are neighbours for,' she said, confirming my guess.

I stood up, needing Carling's helping hand to steady me as I stumbled into a white plastic chair. In the process I also noticed that Clara the midget was missing, unless she was hiding behind the bar again.

'Yes, you're lucky,' Carling said to me. 'If Miss Jerome hadn't called in and we hadn't been close by things could have been rough.'

'Did you catch him?' I asked. 'This prowler.'

He shook his head. 'Gone before we got here but Mullany's taking a look around in case he's hiding some place.'

'He should be easy to spot,' I said.

'Yes,' Terita Montez put in swiftly. 'Over six feet tall, black with an afro.'

Okay, I thought, I've got the message. She was writing my lines in the script for me. 'That's right,' I confirmed, doing my bit to exacerbate black-white relations in Greater Los Angeles.

'And I can't help,' Miss Jerome added. She laughed, a pleasant, musical sound. 'I kept a low profile until I heard the police siren outside.' Even the laugh sounded familiar.

Down at the bottom of the garden a door opened and Officer Mullany came in through the high wall and over towards us. He was as wet as his partner. The crisply clean uniforms would need some sponging and pressing tonight.

'Long gone,' he said when he reached us. He didn't look at me.

'Well, you should be safe now,' Carling told Terita and Miss Jerome. 'You okay?' he asked me.

'I'll survive.'

He nodded, glanced at Mullany, and then the two of them headed out of the garden using the door Mullany had come in by. Terita followed them and bolted the door after they'd gone. I didn't hear if they said anything to one another.

I took another look around while I waited. The jug that had laid me out was missing too, not even a sign of spilled orange juice. Someone was very thorough.

'I must be going,' Miss Jerome said. 'There's been quite enough excitement for one day.'

Something clicked. 'You're Helen Jerome,' I said. 'The film star.'

She laughed her chiming laugh again. 'A long time ago, my dear.'

'It seems like only yesterday,' I said.

'Flatterer.' But I could tell she was pleased to be remembered.

'I saw *Countess from Chicago* three times,' I told her.

'That's twice more than I did.'

'You were very good, and very beautiful. You still are.'

'Thank you,' she said.

Terita Montez was back. We looked at one another in mutual mistrust and dislike.

Helen Jerome said goodbye to us both and went out through the house. Terita saw her out and I followed. The living room was almost the way it had been when I arrived. The difference was a small patch of damp on the polished wood floor at the foot of the stairs. I was standing there, looking upwards, when Terita turned from the door and saw me.

'It's not your ballgame,' she told me.

'What was all that malarkey about a tall, black man with an afro haircut?' I asked.

'Roccisano is a bad man to cross.'

'So people keep telling me. All I came for was information about a young girl whose father wants to know she's safe and well. There's no call for guns and steel bars and people being pushed into swimming pools. To say nothing of telling lies to the cops.'

'I don't know anything about your friend Linda Martin.'

We looked at one another and I knew she was lying and she knew I knew and didn't care a damn.

'I'll be seeing you,' I said and went outside to my car.

'I don't advise it, Mace,' she said.

I grinned at her, climbed in, shut the door with a louder bang than was needed and started the motor. She closed the fancy door and I drove down towards the gates which opened for me. As I turned up the street I saw Helen Jerome disappearing into the garden of the house next door. I thought about stopping to talk to her but decided that this wasn't the best moment. The chances were that someone still had me in view and there was nothing to be gained by endangering old retired movie stars.

It was early evening when I reached the motel and I threw all my wet clothes in a heap in the corner while I showered and shaved and thought and thought.

Having people tell me lies is nothing new, it happens all the time to all policemen everywhere. When those lies are told in such a way that the liar brazenly involves the policeman in their invention, it needs thinking about.

I guessed that I owed a lot, maybe even my life, to Helen Jerome. She'd heard Roccisano's shot and called the cops. With that done Terita had been forced to change the scene, allowing me to live to fight another day. Clearly, she was smart enough to know that I wouldn't kick too much which made her shrewd, which also made her dangerous. It also made her vulnerable, because people as confident as that are prone to making errors of judgement. I would have to lean on her a little and force such an error.

There was no doubt that she was involved; apart from not believing in the coincidence of Linda and Ella going to a party at Terry's, something confirmed not only by both girls independently but also by Maria the Mexican girl, and the telephone number of the Montez house chalked on the kitchen blackboard, I had other things. Terita Montez had known the girls were young, seventeen. Roccisano had been there. The midget had sided with him against me. There was a damp patch on Terita's floor where there hadn't been one before. There was also something else which didn't fit in too readily, not without a shove. I'd already learned that Los Angeles was a hell of a big place to police, yet, of all the cops who could possibly have shown up in answer to Helen Jerome's call it had to be the very same pair who'd arrived at the scene of Ella's murder.

There was another thing about those two cops I didn't like. Both of them had been soaking wet. Getting me out of the water was a job for one man in the pool and one man on the side. Not both men in the pool. However, getting Roccisano out of the pool would have been a very different matter.

All my deliberations did nothing to make me any less worried about Linda's safety. She was mixed up with some very strange and unpleasant characters and the sooner I found her the better I would like it. I was rapidly coming to the conclusion that I would also exceed my original commitment to her father. Persuading her to call home no longer seemed enough; I might have to think about taking her back to England with me. I knew that in one respect it really was none of my business but in another it was. Every time I thought about her I had an unsettling mental picture of my own daughter a few years from now; just as vulnerable and just as far away from home. Maybe, if that ever happened, someone might come along and take care of her the way I was trying to take care of Linda Martin.

I wasn't very hungry and I could still taste chlorine but it was time to eat so I went out and ate, settling for an imitation log cabin drive-in on Moorpark Street. I sat outside on a bench, staring at the passing traffic and eating my fried chicken and wondering what my squad would be doing back home in Liverpool. Probably thinking enviously about me having fun. If only they knew.

I decided that a good night's sleep would do me no harm and headed back for Steele's Motor Lodge. Just in time to see someone coming from my room.

I swung the car in front of another room across the court from mine and waited until the figure climbed into another car and drove off. I couldn't see him too clearly but he was tall and black and had his hair styled in a bushy afro. It looked as though Terita Montez's invention had been given life.

I waited ten minutes, then reparked the car and cautiously opened the door. I risked putting on the light and no bombs went off. I searched the room very carefully and found no sign that anything had gone missing.

Then I searched it again and still found nothing out of place.

So I sat on the bed and thought. Then I switched on the TV and thought some more. That was when I noticed that I couldn't see all the TV picture from where I sat. But I'd sat right in this same position when I'd watched earlier. So, either the bed had been moved or the TV was in a slightly different place.

I checked the bed first, stripping it right down. Clear. I

turned off the TV and used a nail file to unscrew the back. I found a small clear plastic package filled with white powder.

I took it out, went into the bathroom, tasted the powder, then flushed the contents down the toilet. After the cistern had refilled I disposed of the plastic envelope in the same manner.

As I came out of the bathroom the phone rang. I picked it up and spoke my name. The line went dead.

Quickly, I replaced the back on the TV set and switched it on again, then lay down on the bed watching a quiz show in which a lot of overweight women squealed incessantly while trying to win a large automobile with electric everythings.

Five minutes after the phone call they arrived. Plain clothes, big, unsmiling, hard. I let them go through their number, sitting quietly as they searched the room. They were thorough and they were patient. They waited at least eighteen minutes before they took the back off the TV.

I watched their faces and ensured mine remained straight. I knew from personal experience that policemen don't like to be laughed at. I was also learning that policemen don't like to be set up. I was becoming angry.

They spent another half hour after that searching some more but they had lost their enthusiasm for the bust. Something had gone wrong and it was necessary to go back to base and collect another set of instructions.

After they'd gone I turned out the light and undressed for bed, thinking that a change of motel might prove a useful exercise tomorrow, right after I'd kept my nine o'clock appointment with Lieutenant Bercovici.

The morning was overcast with what my car radio told me was early morning smog that would clear by noon. I ate an early breakfast, feeling hungrier than usual and risking a semi-kingsize plate of fried allsorts, then drove over to Lieutenant Bercovici's office.

It was quite a place, making my humble workaday abode back home seem small and grubby and overcrowded. The buidling was new with high-ceilinged rooms, lots of light, and a considerable amount of activity.

A young uniformed officer led me along a corridor, one side of which looked out over the parking lot. An array of flags drooped motionless in the muggy heat and two angry automobiles argued fiercely over the same slot. Apart from the size of the building and the patriotic flag display it was just like home.

Lieutenant Bercovici's office was divided in two by an invisible line. One side was a mess, the other was neat as a new pin. I guessed she shared with a male officer. She had her head bent over a report which seemed to be causing her some trouble.

'Good morning,' I said, to show willing.

She sighed, laid down a pen and looked up at me. She was more beautiful than I remembered. I found myself thinking unproductive thoughts; like, what was she doing for dinner tonight and, how can I fix it so we meet again after all this is over.

'Good morning,' she replied but she was just going through the motions. 'What was all that about yesterday?'

I took it she meant the hassle at Terita Montez's. Officers Mullany and Carling must have reported in, which didn't mean very much in the circumstances. Once Helen Jerome had stuck her innocent little oar in the whole business had been in the open.

I decided there was nothing to gain by keeping secrets from the lieutenant so I told her how and why I'd been there and exactly what had happened. When I was through she stared at me in silence, then fished a sheet of paper from a pile in a tray on the corner of her desk and read it carefully.

'That isn't the way it sounds from this,' she said.

I guessed she was reading the report Mullany and Carling had filed.

'I don't suppose it is,' I said.

Her face stiffened. 'What's that supposed to mean?'

'You tell me, they're your cops, not mine.'

'Officers Mullany and Carling are dedicated men, they both have exemplary records.'

I smiled politely. 'Did you just happen to know that, or have you been checking?'

Her cheeks turned a dusky pink but she held onto her temper. 'Okay, I checked.'

'Why?'

She didn't want to answer that.

'Because they turn up in unlikely places?' I hazarded.

'Partly that,' she admitted reluctantly.

I didn't press for anything more, instead I took the chair from behind the other desk in the room and brought it out front to sit facing her. 'Look, I have no views on police honesty in this town. In my town, yes. I know that even in the best of all possible worlds there are problems. Mullany and Carling are not quite right. You should dig deeper.' Her lips parted but I held up a hand cutting off any response. 'And while you're about it you can also check out two detectives named Carmody and Lewis.'

She frowned.

I told her about the visit last night and the heroin I'd flushed down the toilet.

She stared hard at me for a moment, then abruptly left me sitting there and stalked out of the room. She looked decidedly elegant today. A smart midnight-blue skirt and matching jacket with a lighter coloured high-neck blouse. Her hips had a sway to them that would've been worth millions if it could have been bottled.

Although the office walls were glass I took a chance and reached forward to see what it was she's been reading when I came in. I couldn't make out any details, reading upside-down, but I picked out a few names: Terita Montez appeared to be very well-known in these parts.

When she came back the lieutenant had clearly decided I wasn't paranoid.

'Carmody and Lewis were acting on an anonymous tip-off,' she told me. 'And before you say anything else, they're straight. I worked with Lewis for a year when I was in Narcotics.'

'Okay,' I said. 'So someone wants me out of circulation. We don't have to look far for the reason. I've stood on some toes. God knows what it's all about but that much is certain.'

'All right, Mace. I'll check Mullany and Carling out and put the whole thing up at the top of my case list. Starting with you. What do you think is happening?'

'Something happened the night I saw Linda and Ella. Something that was bad enough for Ella to end up dead and for Linda to go missing.'

'Maybe she's dead too.'

I didn't like to think that way but I couldn't argue. It was a very real possibility. 'Maybe,' I acknowledged.

'What kind of something?'

'God knows. Maybe Terita Montez knows too, and Roccisano. What have you on him?'

'Not much. Came out here from Philadelphia about two years ago. A little drugs dealing, some fixing, providing women for conventions, nothing too heavy.'

I raised an eyebrow. 'What do you have to do around here to be classed as heavy?'

'More than that. Roccisano is strictly small-time. He isn't too bright. He has to be told what to do and how to do it.'

'And who to do it to?'

She nodded her head, causing her long brown hair to fall forward. She brushed it back impatiently.

'In that case,' I said, 'I guess we concentrate on Terita Montez.'

She glanced down at the report. 'I already am,' she said.

'So I'd noticed.'

She frowned, irritated that I was nosy, then managed a smile for the first time since I'd met her. 'I suppose I would've done the same,' she said. 'This something that you say maybe happened that night, what are your guesses?'

'Drugs, I suppose. You say Roccisano's a dealer and someone planted heroin on me.'

She wasn't convinced. 'There's nothing in Montez's file to say she deals. Probably a user but only the way some people use booze.'

She sounded remarkably matter-of-fact about it. Maybe it is something you can grow accustomed to.

'We could use another source.' She thought for a moment. 'Were any other girls working at The Blue Whale?'

'The bartender said he had five.' I thought guiltily about the Mexican girl. I told the lieutenant that by now Maria was probably across the Rio Grande.

She didn't attempt to hide her irritation. 'What about the others?'

'I didn't see any that same night. The following day when I went back I saw a tiny black girl. Maybe calls herself Michelle.'

'I'll talk to her.'

'I'll do that.'

'You're not on the case and even if you were you have no official standing in this country.' She didn't sound too adamant about it.

'But you won't arrest me if I take a ride over to Coliseum Street?' I enquired.

'Be careful,' she said.

'Is that because you secretly care for me?'

Her colour heightened again. 'Because it's my ass on the line if you make waves.'

I grinned. 'And a beautiful one it is too.'

'Get out of here.' she said but she wasn't as angry as she was hoping she sounded.

I went out of the office, along the corridor and out into the parking lot. The flags were twitching in a light breeze that had sprung up and the smog was clearing. It looked as if the forecasters had got it right.

When I reached my car I saw that someone had managed to crush the front wing, cracking but not breaking the headlamp glass.

I drove back to the motel, packed and checked out. Then I drove over to the car rental garage with an idea nibbling at the edge of my mind.

I told the rental people I had been in a slight accident and gave them the number of the black limo I'd seen pick up the bartender outside Carmelo's. They didn't seem too worried but I leaned on them a little, suggesting that if they did find the name of the owner for me I might have a sudden attack of generosity. They agreed to make some phone calls and rented me another car. I told them I would call back about the other car and drove away feeling slightly more secure now I had a different car and would soon have a different address.

The Blue Whale hadn't opened for business yet but I didn't let that little detail stop me. The door in from the alley was heavily barred but an upper floor window looked promising. I used some trash cans to build a shaky pyramid and scrambled up to a point where I could put my elbow through the glass. Moments later I was inside and checking the upper storey. It was mostly empty with those parts that were not serving as storage for beat-up pinball machines.

To get through to the bar I had to kick down a door at the bottom of the stairs. It made a lot of noise but there was no one about to pay much attention.

I checked the office the bartender had said Roccisano used. I went through it fast but thoroughly. I found a notebook with numerous addresses and pocketed it; I also found a list of telephone numbers on the back of a calender hanging on the wall by the phone. Alongside each number was a name. The names included Linda and Ella and Maria. I copied them down on a scrap of paper, then returned the calendar. Then I went down to the girls' dressing-room and searched that too. I came up empty and decided not to push my luck any longer.

Out in the alley I demolished the pyramid of cans and left the scene of my crime.

I drove several blocks until I found a lunch counter. Inside I ordered coffee and spent half an hour going through the address book. None of the entries was written out in full, just abbreviations. Given a couple of days and a street directory I guessed that they could all be deduced. I didn't have the time and, anyway, since the book hadn't been locked away it was a fairly safe bet they weren't too important. I also checked to see if any of the girls' addresses or phone numbers were there. They were not.

I used a payphone at the back of the room to call Lieutenant Bercovici and gave her the numbers, Linda's and Ella's too in case a different address to the one in Burlington Avenue turned up, and also the number of the lunch counter. Half an hour later she called me back. I wrote down what she told me, paid for my coffee and left.

The addresses the lieutenant had given me were all well-scattered. Linda's and Ella's was the one I knew but that left me with three others. Maria's was closest, the other two were over in Boyle Heights and Hyde Park. Their names were Carol and Barbara. Roccisano had mentioned a girl named Michelle. I assumed that she was either Carol or Barbara.

Maria's address was just off Van Ness Avenue and I was there in a few minutes. It was a high old house and from the cluster of illuminated bell pushes by the door it was home for quite a number of people. I still didn't have a second name for Maria but one name among the cluster was M. Carreras. I rang the bell. Nothing; so I tried the door and it opened.

Inside was a shabby hallway with a stairway and two doors. The names on these doors didn't match so I went up the stairs. They were uncarpeted and my footsteps echoed in the dusty stairwell. I could hear the sound of a western movie playing on a TV somewhere. Gunshots vied with galloping music.

M. Carreras lived on the third level. There was no bell so I rapped on the door. The TV accompaniment was louder now, coming from directly across the narrow passage. Paper peeled off the walls and a broken toy baby carriage lay forlornly under the window down at the end. I tried the door but it was locked.

I went down to the end of the passage and opened the window. A rusting fire escape would get me to the window of the room. I was on my way to becoming Los Angeles' most prolific burglar already so there didn't seem much point in stopping now.

From the fire escape I could see into the room. It was almost empty of furniture and what there was looked old and grubby. I used the heel of my shoe to break a small hole in the corner of the window from where I could reach in to release the catch.

Apart from the breaking glass I hadn't made too much noise.

Inside, I took a quick look around the room. There was nothing to tell me that I was in the right apartment in the building. I went into an adjoining room which turned out to be the bedroom. A closet was filled with women's clothes, all cheap and well repaired. A small suitcase was filled with gaudy lingerie including some sparkling g-strings. It looked as if this was Maria's home. It also looked as though she had travelled light when she left town.

One other door opened off the bedroom into what I guessed was a bathroom. I opened the door and stopped dead in my tracks.

Looking at what lay in the bath I had to take a tight hold to stop myself from throwing up.

I've seen death often. I've even caused it. I wasn't prepared for what someone had done to Maria.

When I was reasonably sure I had control over my stomach I stepped inside the bathroom and knelt beside the bathtub.

Her mouth was gagged but her face was unmarked. It was in sharp contrast to the rest of her. Her breasts had been hacked off. From the amount of blood in the bath it was clear that it had been done while she was still alive.

I made myself examine the body, difficult enough already and made worse by the blood which had dried dark brown. I found marks on her upper thighs and the lower part of her stomach. She had been burned with a cigarette end. One of the burnt places was in among her pubic hair. Maria, happy, pretty and strangely innocent when I had seen her last had been tortured before dying a hideously painful death.

I went into the bedroom again and sat on the edge of the bed. Out here I felt even worse. Standing up I took another look around, realising I hadn't seen a phone. I found it pushed under the bed. I used it to call Lieutenant Bercovici. She wasn't in her office but I left a message saying who I was, where I was and that I had a corpse on my hands. I guessed the message would be classed as urgent.

Almost as soon as I'd replaced the phone I heard a police siren wailing closer. In the living room I took a look out of the window and saw a patrol car slide to a stop below me. Two cops, one fat and elderly, the other thin, young and black, climbed out and came into the house. On the way the young one looked up and saw me. Glancing across the street I saw a curtain twitch on the building opposite. I guessed that my breaking and entering had not passed unnoticed.

I was still looking out the window when I heard a door open and quick footsteps on the floor behind me. I started to turn, remembering as I did so that there was another door, probably to a kitchen, I hadn't opened. In my haste I cracked my head on the window frame and was still half-crouched when something exploded above my right ear. I fell to my knees, dimly aware that someone was scrambling past me and out onto the fire escape. There was an impression of legs wearing pants, tight black ones and something gleamed silvery.

Then, with only the faintest feeling that I was getting into some bad habits, I stopped being observant and slid into unconsciousness.

Chapter Four

When I came round the place was filled with cops of all shapes, sizes and colours. I didn't have to make much of an effort to convince them I hadn't touched the girl. I had a bump the size of a mango on the back of my head and anyway the blood on the body was dry. Added to which, I told them I'd reported it all to Lieutenant Bercovici and when she arrived she confirmed that little fact.

Everyone looked a mite green around the gills, especially the lieutenant. She wasn't as tough as she thought she was. And neither was I. Even the police doctor refrained from making jokes the way police doctors everywhere do. Maybe he had a daughter too.

We were outside Bercovici's district but she and the detective in charge had a long earnest conversation during which they looked at me several times and apparently reached some sort of agreement.

Outside, we sat in her car and talked. She wasn't very pleased with me, pointing out, not unreasonably, that I'd broken a couple of laws and if I'd simply sat outside Maria's apartment like any sensible policeman, I would have seen the person who slugged me coming out.

'Maybe, maybe not,' I told her. 'There's a back exit. In any case, I don't suppose it was the killer. My guess is that Maria's been dead about twelve hours. She must've changed her mind about going south. Or someone changed it for her.'

'Why?' she said softly and I knew she wasn't asking why I'd reached that conclusion. She was asking why anyone would torture and murder a young woman in that way.

'Either for kicks or for information,' I said. 'My guess is for information.' I seemed to be doing little more than guess. Facts were few and hard to come by.

'Information?'

'Whoever killed Ella is after Linda. Maria might have known where she is hiding. That why she was tortured.'

'But not that way,' she protested.

'I don't think Maria knew, so she had nothing to tell, so he just kept on going until she was dead.'

The lieutenant shivered slightly and I had a most unpoliceman-like impulse to put my arm around her shoulders. I resisted but mainly because a uniformed cop was guarding the entrance to the apartment house and might have taken it all the wrong way.

'We can't be sure that all this is connected,' she said but from her tone I knew she didn't take her own suggestion very seriously.

'Have you told me everything?' she asked after a few moments of silence.

I thought about that and decided I should tell her about the bartender and the black limousine. I gave her the number and she used her radio to call in and put a trace on it.

'Maybe you should have told me earlier,' she said. 'If it has a bearing, it could be . . .'

Her voice trailed off and I guessed that she had been about to suggest that maybe Maria would still be alive. I was a long way from being sure she was right but I didn't say anything. If she was. it would take a lot of learning to live with.

'I'll call you at the motel when I have something,' she said.

I told her I'd checked out of Steele's Motor Lodge.

'Well, call me when you have a place to stay,' she said.

'Okay, but right now I'm in need of something to stop my nead aching.' I climbed out of her car and walked across to mine.

As I opened up the door she started her motor and slid alongside.

'Follow me,' she said and drove slowly up the street before I had chance to argue.

I followed her and we drove north through narrow streets making turn after turn after turn until I was hopelessly lost but knew that we'd travelled more or less north-west and were somewhere around Century City. Culturally, we were in another world.

Eventually she pulled into a curving, palm tree-lined street with the faintly exotic name of Pandora Avenue. She stopped outside a small, smartly-painted white bungalow with heavy green shutters at the window, a matching green roof and bright red geraniums proliferating all over the place. They sprang from boxes and tubs, from stone pots and hollowed-out logs, and from the garden itself.

As I pulled in behind her the lieutenant climbed out, locked her car door and went up the path. I followed. I guessed we were at her home but I wasn't sure why.

She unlocked the door and went inside. Again I followed on. I was getting quite good at it.

'Sit down,' she told me. 'I'll get something to bathe your head.'

She still hadn't said anything I wanted to argue with so I did that too, dropping into a very comfortable leather and steel armchair. There was a lot of leather and chrome-plated steel in the room. It wasn't masculine exactly, but neither was it especially feminine.

I could hear her clattering about in an adjoining room and a few minutes later she returned carrying a tray with drinks, coffee in beakers and a bowl full of a green-tinged liquid that smelled strongly of antiseptic. She also had a wad of cotton-wool. I slipped my jacket off and dropped it untidily to the floor and let her do her Florence Nightingale number. She was very gentle and from this close up the delicate fragrance of her perfume did alarming things to my pulse rate.

When she was through ministering to my medical needs she handed me a glass.

'Scotch,' she said. 'I take it that's what English policemen drink.'

'Whenever possible,' I confirmed.

'There's cream and sugar for the coffee. Help yourself.'

I spooned in sugar but left it black. 'Thanks,' I said.

'That's okay. You're a long way from home and helping hands.'

'Even if I was at home there would be no helping hands. Except my landlady but she hates men anyway.'

'You're not married?'

'Divorced. Goes with the job.'

She nodded. 'I know.'

'You too?'

'Afraid so.'

'What was his job?'

'The same. Police officer. One trouble was, I outranked him.'

I smiled. 'I guess that made it even worse.'

She nodded, a faint smile coming onto the edges of her mouth. 'How about you?' she asked.

'She just couldn't stand the lousy hours and the moods the job usually put me in when I did get home.'

'Any children?'

I told her about my daughter and her new father.

Out of nowhere a thought strayed into my mind.

'Those telephone numbers I gave you; there were two others apart from Linda's and Maria's. I don't think it's necessary but maybe we should see if those girls are okay.'

'It's done,' she said. 'I radioed in as we drove over here.'

'Then we can relax.' I stretched out, feeling a pain shoot down my neck from where I'd been hit. It must have shown in my face because she reached out a hand with an expression of concern on her face. I took hold of her hand, held it for a moment, then kissed her fingertips. She didn't take it away immediately.

'Obviously, you're feeling better,' she said drily.

I grinned, trying to think of something suitable to say but the moment was spoiled when the telephone rang.

She answered it and spoke quietly for a moment, then listened for much longer.

When she was through she resumed her seat, a puzzled frown etching a line between her arched eyebrows. 'That licence plate number you gave me; you couldn't have been mistaken?'

'No, I'm pretty sure I got it right. Why?'

'It's one of half a dozen vehicles used by members of Vernon Duke's staff. He's front-runner for State Governor.'

I thought about the white-haired, tanned man I'd seen outside The Tail of the Cock. I couldn't see what the bartender from The Blue Whale could have to do with him. Then I saw something else was on the lieutenant's mind.

'The vehicle was reported stolen around ten o'clock Monday night.'

'That's two hours before I saw it.'

'I know.' She paused, worrying over something. 'The theft was reported to two officers in a patrol car,' she added.

'Let me guess. Mullany and Carling.'

She nodded slowly. She didn't like this one little bit. I did; it meant my guess about the two cops being involved in this all the way up to their crisp haircuts was right on the nose.

'Something tells me it's time they were leant on,' I suggested.

Again she nodded her head. I knew the feeling. Finding you have a bent copper on the strength is a cue for strenuous efforts to disprove the fact. Not out of a desire to cover up corruption; it's just that no police officer likes to admit that coppers are only human.

'I'll get onto it in the morning,' she said.

'And until then?'

She looked at me, her eyes showing that her mind was far away.

Standing up I took a short pace until I was beside her chair, then bent down and took her face between my hands and kissed her firmly on the lips. For a moment she remained passive, then she began to participate, then just as swiftly she began to resist. Pulling herself away, she glared at me, anger burning in her deep brown eyes.

'Is that how you show thanks for a kind gesture,' she snapped.

'One way,' I told her.

She wasn't taking it so lightly. 'Dammit, Mace, I was being friendly, that's all. Why did you have to take it as an invitation to go to bed with me?'

She seemed to be unnecessarily wound up. 'Who mentioned bed?' I asked.

She glowered even more grimly and I shrugged, reached down for my jacket and slipped it on. The address book I'd taken from the office at The Blue Whale bumped against my hip. I gave her the book and suggested she might put someone onto deciding if it had any significance. She took it from me but didn't say she would or she wouldn't or even thank you. I really had annoyed her. I was sorry, but I wasn't convinced she hadn't expected it or even been half-prepared to let things roll. She hadn't brought me all this way just to bathe my head. Maybe she'd simply changed her mind. Which was fine by me, just so long as there was a chance she'd change it back again some other time.

I said goodbye and thanked her for the drink and the coffee and the medicare but she didn't want to talk. All she said was goodbye as I went down the path between the masses of geraniums.

I was in my car with the motor running before an image of Maria floated into my mind and I cursed myself for being so bloody insensitive. That must have been it, or at least part of it. The killing had shaken her up and she wanted me with her for no better reason than she didn't want to be alone until she recovered her equilibrium and managed to wash away the immediacy of the Mexican girl's poor, savaged body.

I thought about going back but decided against it. Another time would be best.

I drove away, not sure what to do next but some part of my brain was operating on automatic pilot and soon

I was heading north along Brown Canyon from where I turned into Mulholland Drive, thinking about all the times Philip Marlowe must have driven this way and wondering how he would've coped with a glamorous police lieutenant. Or a dead girl with her breasts cut off.

From Mulholland I turned into Coldwater and I was soon outside Helen Jerome's house in Vedado Avenue.

Like her next-door neighbour, she too had a squawk-box let into the wall beside the gate. We talked through it and she let me in.

The house was smaller and prettier than Terita Montez's glass and flash palace next door. Almost cottage-like in a Californian notion of how Tudor England was supposed to look.

The entrance hall even had a brick-tiled floor and an open fireplace filled with a spray of freshly cut flowers. Brass and copper gleamed everywhere.

Helen Jerome led me into a small, cosy room which looked out into a lawned garden with no sign of a swimming pool. By now the late afternoon sun had completely dispelled all traces of smog and the garden baked quietly. Apart from the sun and the heat I could have been back in England.

The room was panelled in dark wood and was a clutter of photographs and drawings, mostly framed but some pinned to the wall in a wildly jumbled mass. I recognised most of the people in the pictures. Fredric March, Herbert Marshall, Ann Sheridan, Roland Young, Charles Bickford, Frances Farmer, Binnie Hale, Louis Hayward. In most of the pictures, Helen was there too. Stills from her many films. Oddly enough, it didn't look like a museum.

We talked about some of her films and she had a happily wry attitude towards a long-past period in her life that must have contrasted vividly with the life she now led.

After a while she went off to make coffee and I sat and daydreamed about childhood in the cinemas of Liverpool, places that were already falling victim to advancing bingo-calling hordes even as I tried to extend my education. I'd been born a few years too late.

'Come and sit through here,' she called me from the next room. 'This is less of a ghosts' gallery.'

I didn't agree and would happily have stayed there but she insisted. We transferred to a warm, comfortable living room filled with old comfortable wrap-around furniture. She made good coffee. I had the unchivalrous thought that I would rather have been with Lieutenant Bercovici but I stifled it because it wouldn't do any good and, anyway, Helen Jerome was charming and fun and I really had seen *Countess from Chicago* three times because as a small boy I'd been madly in love with her. I didn't tell her that, of course. I'd recovered my lost sensitivity and there was nothing to be gained by telling her that thirty years ago I'd watched her from the front row while still in short pants, at which time she was already past forty and on her fourth marriage.

'Well now, Mr Mace,' she said. 'Thank you for the idle reminiscing but I'm sure you didn't come here to talk about my long-dead career.'

I smiled. 'I wish I had and maybe I can come back and talk again another time.'

'But until then, something more pressing is troubling you?'

I nodded.

'About my neighbour?'

'Yes. Are you friends?'

'Good heavens, no. Dreadful woman. As for Clara. You know she was in the business years ago?'

'Clara?'

'Yes. The studio tried to turn her into another Shirley Temple. They thought they had a winner when they found she wouldn't grow anymore. They could go on forever, or so they thought.'

'What went wrong?'

'Several things. That kind of movie stopped being popular, they found she couldn't act, and then there was the bad publicity.'

'Oh?'

'She had a baby, and killed it. Hacked the poor thing into pieces and tried burning it on a bonfire. It was hushed up after the courts let her off on a technicality.'

'Oh,' I said, thinking about Maria Carreras.

'I've shocked you?'

'Not especially, just given me something to think about. Tell me what you know about Terita Montez.'

'Makes those awful movies. Porno. Even the name is tasteless. I don't object to them for their own sake, it's just that they're so badly made.'

I grinned. 'Anything else?'

She thought a moment. 'No. Sorry.'

'Does she have many visitors?'

'If she does, I don't see them or hear them. Except when she has parties. Wild, noisy affairs.'

'They disturb you?'

'Yes, I tried taking a pill but I don't like such things. Now I just turn the volume up on the TV and watch that all night.' She sighed. 'The trouble with that is all those dreadful old movies. Not that they were dreadful when we made them but now they're cut up for commercial breaks and shortened to fit slots and half the people in them are old friends who have moved into Forest Lawns long ago. It's all too depressing for words.'

'Was there a party there on Monday night?' I asked.

She frowned. 'Odd that. I thought there was one. I heard the noise, music and cars and shouting and laughing. I turned on my TV as usual just as they began showing *Private Worlds*. Claudette Colbert you know. Lovely girl but wouldn't let them photograph her except from the left. It made for some clumsy scenes occasionally.'

'What happened?' I asked patiently.

'Oh, I'm sorry, my dear. I'm rambling, aren't I?' She paused, thinking. 'Well, now, the film began at about eleven.' She broke off again to rummage among a pile of magazines and newspapers beside her chair. She came up with a TV guide and flicked through the pages. 'There,' she said eventually. 'It began at eleven-fifteen. Ran for an hour and three-quarters, what with all the commercial breaks. When it ended at one o'clock I went into the kitchen to make myself some tea and what do you think?'

'The party was over,' I guessed.

'That's right. And usually they go on until five or even six o'clock in the morning. It can't have been a party after all.'

Not unless something happened to bring it to a sudden stop, I thought.

'Does that help you?' Helen Jerome asked.

'I think it does,' I said. 'Although I'm not sure how.'

'Is it something bad?' she asked

I didn't want to frighten her but she seemed to be a pretty spry lady for her age. 'Yes,' I said. 'It is something bad.'

'Well, if there's anything I can do. Watch the house, anything like that.'

I shook my head firmly. 'No, definitely not. There are some very unpleasant people doing some very unpleasant things. Keep out of it, Miss Jerome.'

'Call me Helen, dear and I'll take your advice but, if you need my help just ask. Anything will be brighter than just sitting here watching television and dreaming about the past.'

'Thank you,' I said. 'I'll remember that. And I really will come back and talk some more when all this is sorted out.'

'Whatever it is.'

I smiled. 'Whatever it is.'

She showed me to the door and I kissed her hand because it seemed the natural thing to do; to both of us.

I picked up Mulholland again, driving east, knowing that it was getting late to find a motel or hotel room. I was preoccupied with the day's events and was winding down towards the cluster of lights that marked Hollywood's more densely packed area when I became aware of the car behind me. There was nothing about it that flashed warning signals but warning signals flashed nevertheless.

I turned right onto Coldwater Canyon Drive and the other car did too. Almost at once it picked up speed and came past me. By now it was too dark to see clearly but I had an image of a light-coloured, low-slung saloon with a rumbling souped-up sound to its engine. I carefully slipped off my seat-belt.

Then the car pulled across in front of me and I hit the brakes and swung the wheel to the right and went off the road. The tarmac surface must have been within inches of a steep banking and I went down it like a rally driver but with none of his control. I opened the door and pitched myself out, absurdly thinking about the rental company and the fact that I was going through their cars at an improper rate.

I hit grass and rolled over, bunched up like a parachutist. I stopped rolling and heard my car stop rolling with a sickening crump. Moments later it exploded. I scrambled to my feet, looking down at the flames, feeling sick at the thought of what might have been.

In the light of the flames I could see houses beyond and people running and shouting. Then I heard a sound close behind me and I turned; much too slowly and much too late.

There wcrc two of them, looming shadowy shapes in the darkness. One grabbed me, pinioning my arms by my sides. I kicked out at his companion and felt a satisfying softness followed by an even more satisfying gasp of pain. I didn't have long to enjoy my success.

Strong hands ripped at the sleeve of my lightweight jacket, baring my arm.

The needle hardly hurt at all as it went in. After being hit over the head with a jug of orange juice, then being sapped behind the ear, this was almost therapeutic in its gentleness.

Almost at once the man pinioning my arms changed his grip and then lifted me onto his shoulders as if I were a baby. I tried to struggle but whatever had been pumped into my veins was fast-acting.

I was fully conscious as he carried me up the grassy slope and I knew the man with the needle was walking beside us. But I couldn't even lift my head to see him.

I heard his voice though, calling out to someone that I was alive and they were taking me to hospital and that there was nothing to worry about.

The voice was familiar but I was having difficulty concentrating. I was dumped into a car, slumping across the back seat. Then we were moving off. From someplace I could hear a wailing siren drawing closer. Then I did what I seemed to be doing a lot recently. I passed out.

Chapter Five

I came awake much faster than I'd gone under. All my faculties were present in one flick of an eyelid; head of the list was taste. My mouth tasted like the inside of a tap dancer's practice shoe.

Sitting up I took in my surroundings. I was in a small room, maybe four paces each way with a ten foot ceiling, a small barred window and a door with a peephole in it. The kind for looking in, not out. I was on a bed, iron-framed and hard, covered in a grey wool blanket with a red stripe across one end.

There was no other furniture and no other colour. The walls, ceiling and door were all painted white. Set in the centre of the ceiling was a single electric light made safe by a thick wire mesh. The floor was white thermoplastic tiles.

It wasn't exactly a prison cell, and neither was it exactly a hospital room.

I stood up and stumbled helplessly, grabbing at the bed headrail for support. Sitting down I might have had all my faculties, standing up something was missing. Taking a deep breath, I made a determined slog across the floor to the door. I don't know if it was locked or not. There was no way to find out; no keyhole, no handle. Putting my ear against the door I could hear sounds, very faint. Voices, footsteps, all with a suggestion of an echo.

I tried the window but it was too high off the ground to see over the sill. I tried dragging the bed across to beneath the window but I wasn't up to it so I lay down again and conserved energy.

I thought about the two men who had forced me off the road and drugged me. The voice I'd recognised was that of Officer Mullany so it didn't need too much brain power to deduce that his partner Carling was the man who'd grabbed me. The car trailing me wasn't a prowl car, neither had I seen or felt any suggestion of badges or guns so they must have been out of uniform.

I still didn't know why they were on my case with such determination but one thing was becoming clear, they didn't want me dead. If they did I wouldn't be lying flat on my back in this white box. But someone had wanted Ella and Maria dead. Why was I so favoured?

I lay there thinking for maybe an hour, then made another attempt at heaving the bed across the floor. This time I made it.

Outside it looked to be late afternoon; if that was so I'd been there a fair number of hours. Gently sloping lawns ran down to disappear among brightly flowering shrubs clustered against a high brick wall. A spiked iron rail ran along the wall top. The spikes pointed inwards.

I gave some attention to the window itself. Steel rods at four-inch intervals made it impossible; if I wanted an escape route, and I did, it had to be the door.

Noises outside the window pulled my attention downwards to the ground. I could just make out two men, wearing white coats, wheeling a stainless steel trolley. Then I heard a door opening.

As quickly as I could, I dragged the bed back to its

original position and flopped down on it in time to hear the trolley being trundled inside the building now. The sounds stopped outside my door and a scraping of metal announced someone was using the peephole. I kept my eyes shut and tried to breathe the way I hoped a drugged man might. Then the door opened.

'Still out,' a voice said.

'They used too much, goddamn amateurs.'

'Why should you care?'

'We'll all care if he croaks.'

'You worry too much. What do we do about his food?'

'He can't eat if he's still out.'

'So we'll leave some.'

'No, the Doc doesn't like that.'

'He won't know.'

'Still . . .'

'Do you want to have to come back here at some time in the middle of the night?'

There was a pause. 'Okay, suit yourself.'

I listened to a few assorted rattles and scrapes, then something was dumped on the floor by the bed.

Suddenly, a hand grabbed my arm but it was just a clumsy try at feeling my pulse.

'Seems okay.'

'What did I tell you.'

They went out, dragging their trolley with them and slamming the door. I lay motionless, listening. After what seemed like an hour but was probably less than five minutes, a key turned in a lock. I still didn't move. Several more minutes crawled by with feet as leaden as Ruby Keeler's. Then another scrape announced the closing of the peephole cover. They'd gone.

I risked opening my eyes, then slowly raised my head. They'd left me a tin plate with a domed tin cover. Beside it were knife, fork and spoon. Plastic.

I decided that if I was to get out of here it would be easier with food inside me so after carefully noting the position of the plate I picked it up and lifted the lid. Meat, potatoes and something green that could have been almost anything. The only certain thing about it was that it had been cooked too long. I ate everything on the plate, using my fingers. I'd just finished when I heard sounds outside again. Replacing the cover on the plate I stood it back beside the plastic cutlery and lay back, closing my eyes.

The peephole cover scraped, then scraped back again. The sounds faded and moments later I heard another door close with a muffled bump. Then they were outside again passing beneath my window.

Sitting up I carried out an inventory. Everything I'd had in my pockets seemed still to be there. The only halfway useful things were my plastic credit cards which could be used to open certain kinds of doors, a few coins and the nailfile I'd used on the TV set back at the motel. Someone had been careless; or maybe they knew that a nailfile wouldn't help.

I also had the metal plate and cover and the plastic eating equipment. I eased off the bed and searched the room in case I'd missed anything the first time. I hadn't. One thing the exercise proved, I was steadier on my feet now.

I spent a fruitless twenty minutes feeling all the way around the edge of the door, using one of my credit cards. I found the hinges and the lock. There was no way I would get out of there with anything I had; a small explosive charge might have helped but not much less than that.

That left me with the window, or a surprise attack on whoever came in next.

The window seemed as hopeless as the door but then

I crawled under the bed and spent a few more minutes examining it in detail.

It took maybe a couple of hours but when I'd finished the bed looked exactly as it had to start with from above. The only difference was that it wouldn't take any weight. I'd removed most of the supporting members and arranged them neatly against the door to the lock side. I hadn't seen the door when it was opened but assumed that it opened outwards. That being so, anything leaning against the wall on the hinge side would be in direct line of vision of anyone coming in.

With my armoury so arranged I set to work on the window. One of the struts from the bed, leant against the wall beneath the opening, gave me a shaky lift to enable me to work on the protecting bars. The metal plate, folded with a great deal of effort into a scoop, provided me with a tool.

I kept at it for an hour but had made no progress; not even one bar was loose, besides which I kept falling off the strut.

I abandoned the task, putting the strut with the other potential weapons and replacing the more or less reshaped plate with the cover and the cutlery. Then I curled up on the floor beside the bed, covered myself with the grey and red blanket and went to sleep, hopeful that I would be alert to any sounds.

I was, even though my watch told me I'd slept about six hours.

The sound that woke me was, of all things, someone scratching at the window from the outside.

That threw me but as there was nothing I could do about it, I stayed quiet, listening, Then I heard a whisper. Whoever was outside was calling my name.

I decided to take a chance. I scrambled to my feet,

picked up one of the bed struts and tapped against the window.

'That you, Mace?' a man called softly. I didn't recognise the voice.

'Yes.'

'Let me see you, make sure you're the man.'

I thought about that for a moment. Somehow, putting my head in the window with the light behind me didn't seem like a very bright idea. 'I can't reach,' I called, trying to hold my voice down to a soft but audible whisper.

The voice mumbled something which could have been, Shit, but I wasn't sure.

Then I heard footsteps moving away and moments later a door opening. Whoever it was was coming the same way as the dinner-servers had done.

I took a quick look at the peephole, then stepped off to one side just in case. I had a feeling that I was letting myself become paranoic but even paranoids have enemies and right now I wasn't prepared to trust anyone.

Moments passed, then the peephole cover scaped. I waited.

'Can't see you,' the voice said.

He couldn't look and shoot at the same time but when I let him see me I kept moving just in case.

Then the lock turned.

I moved fast and smooth, sweeping up one of the bed struts. All my precautions seemed well-founded when the first thing I saw come peeping into my little room was the muzzle of a large calibre revolver.

I didn't hesitate, bringing the steel strut down on the gun as hard as I could. There was a yell, a metallic clatter, then I was reaching for the arm and pulling the man inside. I hit him once with the end of the strut, right in the stomach. He went down with all the grace of a stunned ox.

I picked up the gun, then stepped over the body and took a look outside. A long and wide corridor lit by lamps similar to that in my room stretched in both directions. Other doors like mine lined both sides. About six paces along, on my side, was a wired-glass door. I guessed that led to the outside. A bunch of keys hung from the one that had turned the lock in my door. I pocketed them, then propped my door open, carefully wedging it with the bed strut. I didn't want the door accidentally swinging close on me.

Back inside my little cell I examined my saviour. He was tall and black and had an afro-styled haircut. I couldn't be sure, not having seen him clearly before, but my guess was he was the man who had planted the heroin in my TV set back at Steele's motel.

He was groaning and retching, then he came suddenly to his feet, his hands grabbing at me. I stepped back and showed him his gun. He stiffened, then tried a smile.

'That's a hell of a way to greet the guy who's rescuing you from this joint,' he said.

He was right, it was a hell of a way to act. 'Thanks,' I said. 'Sorry if I hurt you but until I know who sent you and why we keep things the way they are.'

His eyes narrowed slightly but the smile remained. He had high cheekbones which gave him a curiously Slavic look. 'Okay,' he agreed.

'We'll go out the way you came in, unless you've any better ideas,' I said.

He nodded and I stepped backwards into the corridor, taking care I kept every part of him in view. I didn't want him using one of my bed struts on me.

I was right about the exit door and soon we were

heading across the grassy lawn I'd seen from the window. By now it was black as pitch and only reflected light from the building gave us any help. At the bushes the big man turned right and moved fast and softly along the wall. When he stopped I thought he was planning trouble but we'd reached another building.

A window threw bright light out into the darkness. He glanced in and after a moment so did I. Two men in white coats were slumped over a table. A half dozen stainless steel trolleys were lined up against a wall. I guessed these were my meal servers. I also guessed that they were not sleeping the sleep of the hard working. My saviour had put them out. It crossed my mind that it might be permanent but one of the men moved, stirring gently in his unexpected rest.

Afro moved on again and I followed. The next time he stopped I could see we were in a parking lot. He gestured towards the parked vehicles and, like an idiot, I looked the way he was pointing.

He grabbed for the gun, bringing a knee up into my groin. I managed to twist sideways, taking the heat of the blow on my hip. I also managed to hang onto the gun. He was big and he was tough. Given an even match we might have had quite a tussle but with me still a mite shaky from the drugs, it was no-contest. So I evened the odds. I hit him once, hard along the jawbone with the barrel of his gun. Then I hit him again, across the other side of his jaw. I heard something crack and he went down.

I knelt beside him, lifted his wallet and a set of car keys, but then I decided that with over fifty cars in the parking lot I couldn't spare the time to find out which was his. I dropped the keys onto his chest and went in search of the way out.

The exit was through big, locked gates just beyond

the parking lot. I still had the keys the big man had used to open up the cell and I tried them all on the locks but with no success. Then I saw headlamps approaching and moments later a sleek white ambulance arrived outside the gates.

There was just one man in the cab and he came out from behind the wheel to climb down and unlock the gates for himself. I was all set to walk through when it crossed my mind that I didn't know where I was or how far I had to go to reach safety. Wherever I was and however far I had to travel, wheels would help.

Moving forward fast, I reached the ambulance driver and tapped him gently but hard enough to ensure he was out for as long as I needed.

Moments later I was in the ambulance, swinging it around in a clumsy three-point turn in the narrow roadway outside the gates. As I turned the lights caught a sign on the wall. I had been a guest of the Meridian Home for the Mentally Handicapped.

I wondered if I was hi-jacking a patient who was destined for the funny-farm. If I was I hoped it wasn't a paranoid. This would be enough to give his delusions delusions.

My lights picked up a tall figure shakily trying to scramble into a car. Afro was about to take off. I didn't wait to see if he made it, instead I hit the accelerator pedal and shot off along the road faster than was safe at any time least of all in darkness on unfamiliar roads in a strange vehicle and with God knew what kind of stuff still pumping around in my veins.

I risked a glance around the cab. A wired-glass panel was let into the bulkhead behind me but it was dark in the back of the ambulance and I could see nothing. There was probably a light switch somewhere but there was no time to look for it.

It was about twenty minutes before I reached a busy road and a further ten after that before I picked up a road sign that looked at all familiar. I had made several precautionary turns and had completely lost my bearings, not that I'd known which side was up to begin with. However, now I was coming into San Bernardino from the north.

I drove on steadily, I didn't want to pick up an inquisitive traffic cop, and eventually passed the freeway. I followed signs to TriCity Airport and left the ambulance in the short-stay parking zone. Just before I walked away from it I listened at the rear door but didn't hear anything. I hoped I hadn't taken a new inmate of the Meridian Home for an unscheduled ride; I already had enough on my plate without adding to the instability of someone with that kind of problem. To be safe, I used a payphone to call airport security and tell them where they could find the ambulance. That done I joined a small line of people waiting to buy bus tickets for the ride into LA.

The clerk looked at me curiously but said nothing. I took the hint and went into the men's room. The mirror on the wall told me that I was far from being the fairest thing around. Deep yellow and blue shadows under my eyes blended into a surprisingly heavy growth of stubble on my chin.

I made use of machines vending disposable razors and ready-pasted toothbrushes and tried improving my appearance. I didn't look much healthier but at least I didn't look as if I was an escapee from a funeral home.

On the way out I bought a newspaper for something to hide behind in case the need arose. When I was on board the bus my first glance at the paper told me why my whiskers had grown so much and also explained some of my weakness when I'd first woken up. It wasn't

Thursday, it was Friday. I'd been in the Meridian twenty-four hours longer than I'd thought.

Sitting there, as the bus pulled out of the airport, I knew I had added to my problems in a way which also exacerbated the bind Linda was in. There was a curious dichotomy in the way people were acting towards me. While everyone I ran into seemed eager to take a swing at me, some were willing to settle for the relative friendliness of rendering me merely unconscious; others wanted me dead.

Roccisano and the black guy with the afro I'd left behind at the Meridian Home came into the fatally-inclined category; whoever had bopped me on the head in Maria Carreras's apartment belonged to the less violent group along with Mullany and Carling. The fact that I'd been dumped in the mental hospital suggested that all they wanted was to keep me out of the way for a while.

The bus was bowling briskly along the San Bernardino freeway and the sky behind us was beginning to lighten with a brand-new day. I showed my appreciation of that fact by falling asleep.

When I awoke we were deep in the heart of the City of the Angels and I stared out the window at the passing streets and buildings and vehicles and people, thinking about the number of times Philip Marlowe must have driven through these not so mean streets. I wondered if he would still recognise his town or if things had changed too much since then.

We slid through a brash, high-sided canyon of office buildings and shopping malls all agleam with black glass and gilded flagpoles, past an early-morning drunk who was all tangled up with a newspaper that had blown about his legs and was threatening to upend him, past the roadside benches painted bright with slogans advertising a Jewish funeral home, on past a record store just opening for business with a thin black youth in brown uniform standing guard at the door and trying to be unselfconscious about the heavy-calibre revolver strapped around his waist, then on past the fancy shops with entrance lobbies so huge the Taj Mahal would have brushed neither sides nor ceiling. Then we were among the tourists staring bright-eyed at those sights they'd always dreamed about and mingling with them the kids from all corners of the land staring dead-eyed at dreams that had turned sour and which only booze or drugs or prostitution might, they hoped, bring back to life, and up among the hills beyond were the luxury mansions still touted by the tour operators as the Homes of the Stars but which were now home to oil-slick Arabs and computer whizz-kids from Silicon Valley and their silicone-implanted plastic-replica wives, and even further on and up into the mountains lay the ranches and palaces of superstars of films and records and business and politics which together still conspired to uphold the faded and tattered belief that this was the Land of Opportunity and that anyone could achieve the American Dream.

Curiously enough, in spite of all the evidence to the contrary, it was difficult to sustain cynicism for long. Perhaps Philip Marlowe would still have recognised it after all; it was only the soft centre of hope buried beneath his thick cynical carapace that kept him going.

I finally hopped off the bus bang in the heart of Century City and risked walking through the already hot streets the half mile or so to Pandora Avenue.

I was in sight of Lieutenant Bercovici's display of red-petalled geraniums when it crossed my mind that she would probably not be there at this time of day. But then I saw her car in the driveway and knew at long last luck was coming my way.

When she opened the door to find who was ringing her bell she stood for what seemed like an age staring at me. I guess I was still not a very pretty sight.

'You'd better come in,' she said eventually. 'Unless you plan on collapsing on the doorstep.'

I negotiated the step, feeling instantly better in the cool and sweetly scented interior of her house. 'I don't feel as bad as I look,' I told her.

The first full-scale smile I'd seen from the lieutenant came onto her face. 'Nobody could feel as bad as you look,' she assured me. 'Sit down and I'll fix you a drink.'

I did as I was told; even if I'd wanted to argue, which I didn't, I couldn't have done so. Reaction against the past hours was catching up with me.

She brought me Scotch again, then dropped gracefully into the leather and steel chair I'd sat in last time I was here. I'd settled for a plain cream hide settee in case I was overtaken by the need to sleep.

She was dressed casually today, which in her case meant much smarter than the average lady of leisure. Tight grey trousers in some soft material with a thin pink and grey-striped sweater that showed off her figure considerably better than anything I'd seen her wear before. She had nothing on her feet and the loss of the three inches extra height her shoes usually gave her contrived to make her appear more vulnerable. Or maybe that was wishful thinking.

'I expected to hear from you', she said. 'I take it you've been busy.'

'In a manner of speaking.'

'What was it? Wine, women and song?'

'Or in my case, booze, broads and big band music.'

'If you say so.'

I shook my head. 'None of those.' I hesitated. She

wasn't going to like this, not with Officers Mullany and Carling having a hand in the action.

Then, careful not to leave anything out and equally cautious about putting in anything I wasn't sure about, I told her what had happened to me.

She listened to me carefully, not interrupting, not commenting, her face serious and concerned. When I'd finished she didn't speak for a few moments and when she did went off at an unexpected tangent.

'You must be hungry, what would you like to eat?' she asked.

Surprisingly, or maybe not so surprisingly, I was. 'Anything,' I told her.

'In this house we don't eat anything, only the best that a cordon bleu course at junior high can offer.'

'We?'

'My daughter and I.'

'Oh.'

She laughed lightly. 'There was a wealth of unstated emotion in that syllable.'

'Isn't that something you make with cream?'

'What?'

'Syllable.'

'Idiot.'

Standing up, she stood for a moment looking down at me. 'More Scotch?' she asked.

'Not right now, thanks.'

She went out of the room and after a moment I followed her into the small but exceedingly well-equipped kitchen at the back of the house.

'How old is your daughter?' I asked.

'Sixteen.'

I looked at her, doing sums in my head.

She saw the look and laughed again. 'I'm thirty-three, my daughter came very early.' She was abruptly serious. 'She was born when I was her age now. The same age as your Linda Martin and Ella Streeter and only a couple of years short of Maria Carreras.'

'We're not supposed to take a personal angle in our work,' I remarked.

'I know, but it doesn't always happen that way, does it?'

I shook my head.

She turned away and began taking things out of cupboards and generally acting like an ordinary home-loving woman and not like a detective investigating a case that had all the outward signs of a very nasty business.

'I'll make arrangements for Mullany and Carling to be put on ice,' she said. 'Nothing too heavy, just a temporary transfer to duties that will keep them out of the way until we know exactly what is going on.'

'Good idea.'

'I'll also have someone take a look at the Meridian Home. I'm not too sure what we can do about the guy with the gun who tried to kill you.'

'I only think he was trying to kill me.'

'Whatever. You'd know him if you saw him?'

'Sure.'

'Well, maybe we can take a look at the mugshots file.'

'Right.'

I noticed that she seemed to be getting nowhere with the culinary arrangements. She was just standing things down, then picking them up and standing them someplace else. I looked at her face. Her colour was higher than normal and her eyes a touch brighter. I realised that my pulse rate was up a few notches.

'What time will your daughter be home?' I asked.

'She's away, staying with my parents up in Oregon. It's school vacation time.'

'This is your day off?'

She nodded, not looking at me.

'And no visitors expected.'

'For God's sake, Mace, what the hell do you need?'

'The last time I was here I kissed you and you damn near threw me out on my ear.'

She came across the kitchen towards me, went up on her bare toes and put her arms around my neck. 'There are wrong times and there are right times,' she said softly.

I didn't see much point in asking if my guess that she'd been upset over seeing Maria's body was the cause; it was pretty obvious she had been. It was equally obvious that I was wasting valuable time. I bent towards her and kissed her lips which parted as though she was taking the first drops of water after a long stay in the desert.

When she eventually pulled away it was only to take my hand and lead me through the house and up the stairs. Neither of us spoke.

Her bedroom was much more feminine than the room downstairs. I guessed that this was what she was really like, the living room a display of her police officer's shell. Most visitors wouldn't get beyond that point and would remain impressed that she was just as tough as she made out.

We kissed again and I could feel her body shaking. 'What is it?' I asked.

'It's been a long time,' she whispered. 'In my position, care and caution is needed otherwise people come to the wrong conclusions.'

'Then we'd better make up for the long, dry spell.'

'Will you, for heaven's sake, stop talking and start acting.'

I did as I was ordered.

She was wearing nothing beneath the pink and grey sweater and her breasts were soft and as beautiful as her face, their nipples dark brown and already aroused. I kissed them, then nibbled gently at first one, then the other. I felt her hands pulling at my shirt.

'I could do with a bath or a shower,' I told her. 'Two days in the loony-bin hasn't done much for my bodily hygiene.'

'In there,' she said.

The bathroom adjoined the bedroom and by the time we'd reached it we were both naked and beginning to learn a great deal more about one another.

The shower was hot, thankfully so, and I could feel the sweat and grime of my exertions washing away. She was with me under the fine hot spray and the lather we worked up on our bodies wasn't all down to the scented soap.

We took towels into the bedroom and when we were dry there was no part of either of us that had gone unexplored and caressed and kissed.

When, at last, perhaps an hour or more after we had left the shower, I finally entered her it was as smooth and as soft and as warm and as right as if we had been made for each other. In fact it was so right I wouldn't have been at all surprised if I'd woken up to find I was still in my white cell and the drugs only just wearing off.

I'm no monk, but with no permanent woman in my life there were long stretches without sex. This was the end of one such period; for her it was clearly the end of a much longer drought.

When I had held out as long as I could she was already up to her fourth body-wracking orgasm. It had been good and the explosion as I finally threw off all restraint was almost audible.

A long, warm and comfortable silence followed as

we continued to touch and stroke those surfaces we were already learning held most pleasure for the other.

She was the first to break it. 'Are you always that good?'

Like most policemen I can tell a convincing lie when I have to. I didn't have to then, more to the point I didn't want to. 'No,' I admitted.

'I'm glad,' she said.

'Oh?'

'That makes it something special for us.'

I knew what she meant. My eyelids were growing heavy.

'Don't tell me you're falling asleep,' she said.

'Men always do, it's part of the pattern.'

'The hell with the pattern. I expect a repeat performance.'

I groaned theatrically.

Then she slid her long legs off the bed and stood up. 'But first I'd better do what I started out to do and fix you something to eat.'

'Better mix in some ground rhinoceros horn.'

'That is the last thing you need.' She was slipping on a dark brown velvety robe. 'Don't go away,' she commanded.

'I couldn't if I wanted to, and I don't.'

I listened to her going down the stairs, doing something almost unladylike and whistling a song I didn't recognise. Then I could hear pots and pans being clattered about and then I couldn't hold out any longer and fell contentedly asleep.

My last clear thought before I went completely out was one of guilt that in the middle of all that was happening, and with Linda's fate still uncertain, I was happier than I'd been in years.

Chapter Six

Saturday was a working day for Lieutenant Bercovici but somehow we managed to forget that fact until almost ten o'clock.

The previous night we'd eaten well, she really was far above mere cordon bleu standard, and drunk sparingly and had somehow made our first efforts at lovemaking fade into near insignificance. It had been a magnificent night.

Finally, we were both fully dressed for what seemed like the first time in weeks and she was ready to leave for the day's slog.

I pointed out that not only was I without transport but I'd also lost all my luggage in the car when it went up in flames.

She offered to drop me off where I could buy some basic needs and also a change of clothes and we arranged to meet for lunch around one. That also gave me time to go over to the car rental agency and explain what had happened to the second car I'd had from them.

They expressed considerable misgivings about letting me try for a hat-trick but I gave them Lieutenant Bercovici's name and number and they called her and seemed satisfied that I wasn't some kind of nut with a car-wrecking complex.

As I filled in all the necessary papers one of the people I'd spoken to before came in. 'I got that information for you,' he told me. 'The owner of the limo you tangled with is Vernon Duke.' He said the name with a touch of awe.

I thanked him politely, not thinking it necessary to tell him I already knew.

'The guy said he was sorry you'd had trouble but you were welcome to compensation if you cared to call,' he went on.

I frowned at that. 'You spoke to him?'

'Not in person, one of his people. Any reason I shouldn't?'

There was no reason, it just hadn't occurred to me he would go that far. But there had been no accident, I'd made it all up. So what was all this nonsense about compensation.

'You gave my name?' I enquired.

He nodded, a worried frown creeping onto his face. 'Did I do wrong?'

I had a feeling he had done wrong and that at least one part of my adventure out at the Meridian Home for the Mentally Handicapped was a direct result of that wrongdoing but I didn't say so. 'Of course not,' I assured him. 'Maybe I will call,' I said. 'What was the name of the man you spoke to?'

He scratched around among a thousand pieces of paper until he came up with the right one. 'McQuaid,' he said. He handed me the piece of paper which also had a telephone number on it.

I thanked him and put the scrap of paper in my pocket. This was something I needed to think about.

It was almost one by the time I was in my new car

and I headed straight for my lunch date with the lieutenant. I'd changed my clothes at the store where I bought the new outfit and was smarter than I'd been when I left her but I needed a shave. I was first to arrive at the restaurant and took advantage of that fact by shaving in the men's room with the aid of my new razor. I wondered how long the insurance company would take to sort out all the claims. One way and another this holiday, if it ever became a holiday, was proving expensive and not just financially. I was also taking my share of physical and emotional battering.

When the lieutenant arrived we ordered from a menu that made up in cost what it lacked in variety and sat at the bar waiting for our table to be made ready. The restaurant was small but classy, in keeping with its tariff. Named the Carlton, it stood on Sunset across the street from a splendid old building that looked as if it really belonged. I said as much to the lieutenant.

'It's the Hollywood Athletic Club,' she told me. 'Or rather, it was back in the Thirties. A publishing company has it now. They spent a fortune on it, restoring it to just the way it was. There's even a pool in the basement where Johnny Weismuller used to swim.'

'Maybe that's why they put the two stone lions out front; to make him feel at home.'

'Who knows, stranger things happened here way back when.'

'Do you like it here?'

'It's okay.'

'But not as much as Oregon?'

'How do you know about that?'

'You told me that was where your daughter was, staying with your parents. I am a detective.'

'So you are, I keep forgetting.'

I looked at her admiringly. She was wearing the skirt

she'd worn the first time I saw her but this time with a high-necked army-green sweater. 'I have to admit I find it hard to remember you're a cop.'

She leaned forward and let me kiss her.

'I think we should talk shop,' I said. 'Otherwise I might well commit an indecent act in public.'

She grinned at me. 'Okay; for now. We've nothing new on the girls. No one's made any attempt to get close to either of the other two dancers from The Blue Whale but that might be due to nothing more than the fact that we have them under surveillance. There's still no sign of Roccisano, Terita Montez seems to be staying home and keeping quiet and if her companion is still at the house she's keeping out of sight.'

'Companion?'

'Clara King.'

'Ah, the midget lady with the mean left hook. How about the Meridian?'

'Seems to be straight, or at least we've had no complaints until now. I'm having a check run on the people who own it.'

I stared into my drink.

'Worried because you're not doing anything?' she asked.

I grinned and nodded my head.

'There isn't much you can do, except maybe look at mug shots in the hope of identifying the man with the afro haircut and the gun.'

'Shit,' I said.

'What does that signify?'

'His gun. I took it away from him.' I thought for a moment. 'I must have left it in the ambulance. Maybe too late but you could call the security cops at TriCity airport and ask them if they still have the vehicle to take a look. Try for prints on the cartridge cases, those on the outside will be mine. Maybe even a number but I have a feeling he was a professional.'

She slid off her stool as the waiter approached to tell us our table was ready. 'I'll call in right away,' she said.

I went with the waiter and along the way I decided that there was something I could do this afternoon but was in two minds whether or not to tell Lieutenant Bercovici as it involved a slight case of larceny.

By the time she rejoined me at the table, after threading her way elegantly through the other tables that crowded the restaurant's small room, I had decided to tell her if only because I wanted her with me where, if the need arose, I could hold her hand.

Surprisingly enough she agreed although I had a feeling her motives for coming along were very similar to my own and that at any other time she wouldn't have overstepped the bounds of legality.

We left her car in the Carlton parking lot and drove in mine up Coldwater Canyon Drive, past the burnt-out hulk of my previous car which at that moment happened to be trailing up the grassy slope behind a caterpillar-tracked tow truck, and eventually emerged on Ventura. Soon we were heading north on Van Nuys way beyond Carmelo's.

We passed the junction with Chandler Boulevard which gave me a nice warm glow before the lieutenant spotted Terita Montez's studio in the block between Gilmore and Hamlin Streets.

Most of the other buildings were home to small businesses: a couple of panel-beaters, a spray shop, a coffin-maker, a slot-machine repair shop, a film processing lab., a recording studio, a car customiser who advertised his trade with the front end of a 1956 Chevy Bel-Air bursting through the front wall all aglow with gold-dust paint and purple and lime-green lettering. With a sign like that I wouldn't have trusted him to paint the lieutenant's left little finger nail.

All the businesses except one were closed; Saturday afternoons in this town are not for working. The exception was the coffin-maker. Some trades have no slack periods.

I left Lieutenant Bercovici out front while I went around back of the building and compounded all the other felonies I'd committed in the past few days. No one heard me break glass as I timed it to coincide with hammer blows from the coffin-maker. It seemed only fair to use him to help me. The way things were going, he and his kind were benefiting from my visit to their fair city.

Once I was inside I went straight through to the front, checking for burglar alarms as I went but there were none to be seen. I opened up the front door and beckoned the lieutenant inside.

We drew a blank in the office and the studio didn't improve the score. So far as I could see the place was a single-room set equipped with a king-size bed, a couple of pieces of furniture to make it look less like a studio and more like someone's bedroom, and a set of lights that would ensure none of the finer detail was missed during filming.

'How about a film test?' I enquired, glancing at the bed.

'Don't,' she said.

I suppose it was a tasteless remark in the circumstances.

I took another look around and came upon what looked like a cupboard door. I was about to open it when I spotted a thin wire tight in around the door surround. I traced the wire to where it ended up among a collection of miscellaneous pieces of electrical switchgear.

Lieutenant Bercovici was watching me with interest. 'What have you found?'

'I think it's a burglar alarm,' I said.

It was. It took me a while to figure out how it worked. There was nothing too sophisticated about it and took only moments to disconnect. Then I went back and opened the cupboard door. It turned out it wasn't a cupboard, it was the entrance to a cellar.

I went down cautiously, felt around until I found a light switch, then called the lieutenant down.

'You know they could have my badge for this,' she said when she joined me.

'If they do I'll find you a job directing traffic in Dock Road, Birkenhead on Saturday afternoons.'

I walked the length of the cellar. On both sides of the long narrow room were glass-fronted cabinets all chockful of cans of film and video cassettes. It looked as if we had found Terita Montez's pornographic film library.

Everything was neatly numbered and another few minutes searching, this time in drawers beneath the cabinets, produced a large leather bound ledger which was the catalogue file. In here the numbers corresponded to titles with various letters appended. The titles showed a marked lack of imagination but I suppose anyone's inventiveness would have dried up after trying to find something new to label similarly sexually explicit productions. The titles helped in one thing, they tied in with the letters and gave a rough guide to the code. Such appendages as 'sm' were easy enough, others were harder to figure out but one thing was abundantly clear. Terita Montez catered for every possible taste.

It was also apparent that these were the master copies and that from them copies were made, often in large numbers.

'It's all legal, you know,' the lieutenant told me. 'Unless what they're doing on the film is against the law but even then it's the act not the film that breaks the law and we have a hard time making charges stick.'

I wasn't paying too much attention. Laws against porno films were not something I could heat up over. Where paths crossed I carried out the law, even if some of the time I didn't think I was serving any great social need.

After a moment I had an idea. Walking along the cabinets I followed the numerical sequence. It took time but it was worth the effort although I didn't know if I had achieved anything much. Two numbers in the sequence were missing. I checked the ledger. Both were films, not videos and both had the same letter appended. A letter 'l'. I'd already concluded that meant lesbian in Terita's code. It could have been coincidence and I might be chasing after windblown straws but I wondered if the missing films were of Linda and Ella doing their 'act'. I told Lieutenant Bercovici what I was thinking.

'If you're right, where does it get you?'

'Maybe nowhere,' I conceded.

'So now what?'

I'd already decided what I wanted to do next but I had also regretfully concluded that I couldn't justify asking her to take any more risks with her job.

I put everything back the way it had been when we came down into the cellar, then went back up the stairs. I reconnected the burglar alarm. Soon after that we were back out front sitting in my car. I told the lieutenant what I wanted to do.

'Dammit, Mace, how many laws do you plan to break?'

'Only as many as is necessary,' I assured her.

She grumbled some more but eventually agreed.

We drove back to the Carlton and her car. She didn't get out right away. 'Be careful,' she said.

I grinned.

She leaned across and kissed me harder than was necessary. 'Idiot,' she said.

She climbed out, then looked back inside. 'Do you realise, I don't even know your first name?'

'I don't know yours.' I laughed. 'It's about the only thing I don't know about you.'

Her colour darkened and she looked even more beautiful than ever. 'Well?' she demanded.

'What?'

'What's your name, dammit?'

'Like I told you the first time we met, you can call me sweetheart.'

She slammed the door.

Leaning over I wound down the window. 'What do I call you?' I called.

She glanced back. 'Like *I* told *you*, you can call me Lieutenant.' She was trying to look angry, but she was laughing.

I watched as she drove out of the parking lot and waved as she headed back the way we'd just come to do her part of the next operation.

Twenty minutes later I parked the car in someone's driveway just beyond the point where Vedado Avenue joined Alta Mesa Drive, slid down low in my seat and checked the time. Five more minutes and Lieutenant Bercovici would be calling Terita Montez with a report that her studio had been burgled and she was needed to identify any losses.

It was quiet, unnaturally so and the sun was gone behind looming black clouds.

Two cars passed, both driven by men with no

passengers. There was no guarantee this would work, maybe Terita would send someone else, or just refuse to go. The fact that she had stayed close to her house for the past few days had to have motivation. Whatever it was, it might outweigh her business instincts.

It was even darker now and suddenly giant drops of rain fell ponderously out of the sky, exploding on the roof of the car. Seconds later the clouds opened and a genuine LA flash storm turned the scene into an approximate equivalent of the interior of an automatic car-wash. I could see nothing outside, just the thick stream of water pouring over the windows. To make matters worse the inside of the car began steaming up.

Winding down the window I risked a soaking in order to see what, if anything came up the road. I didn't hear it, but moments later a car nosed cautiously up the hill, wipers furiously attempting to clear water from the windscreen.

I might have failed to identify the driver but she had her face pressed forward against the glass, straining to see ahead. It was Terita Montez. I was in business.

As soon as she was out of my sight I started up the motor and eased forward down the hill. Mud was washing across the road, swept down from surrounding gardens by the weight of water. I could understand how sometimes houses came adrift in such storms.

I parked the car around the back of Helen Jerome's house, took a deep breath and ran for the gate that led into the garden of the Montez house. It was bolted from the inside but it proved a sort of ladder to allow me to scramble up and over the wall into which it was set.

By the time I dropped down into the garden I was soaked to the skin, my new clothes well on the way to being ruined. But the odds were in favour of no one having seen me.

Up by the pool, I sheltered a moment beneath a sun awning. The wind and rain were turning the surface of the pool into a miniature of how the Atlantic might look in a Force Ten.

I couldn't be sure there was no one in the house. Maybe Clara the midget was there, lurking in some shadowed corner with a baseball bat; or maybe Roccisano was watching me right this minute and planning on which of my legs he would break first. But, equally, I couldn't hang around indefinitely. Without waiting for reason to prevail, I picked up a piece of steel tubing that could have been the one Roccisano tried to brain me with and which I could now see was part of a dismantled springboard and smashed the glass in the big sliding patio window.

Inside the house I had taken two steps when an alarm went off. It was a high decibel shrieker, the kind that guarantees to scare any interloper out of his wits, or if he stays to give him a severe case of the Quasimodos. If it hadn't been for the storm raging outside, half of Studio City would have been down on me.

The gadget was on a cupboard, hidden behind a framed photograph of Clara. I turned it off and stood for a moment letting the ringing in my ears subside a little. I still had the piece of tubing in my hand and I decided to keep it with me just in case.

I carried out a hasty recce of the house, found no one hiding inside or under anything, then began a systematic search. I didn't know what I was looking for, I just hoped that I would know it when I found it.

The ground floor produced nothing at all. The large living room occupied most of the floor area, with only a small kitchen and a utility room I hadn't seen before. I didn't waste much time on either.

Upstairs were three bedrooms, one with an attached

bathroom, a separate bathroom and a tiny photographic darkroom. The floor area was bigger than down below because it extended out above the garage.

I started with the darkroom but came up empty. One of the bedrooms was obviously Terita's, another equally obviously was Clara's. The third room appeared to be for guests but if anyone had stayed recently he or she had left no trace. Neither of the bathrooms gave me anything and I was sadly coming to the conclusion that I had wasted time and effort and had a soaking all for nothing. Then the telephone rang. There was an extension in Terita's bedroom. I walked towards it, listening and counting the rings. It didn't stop but kept on ringing. I stood in the passageway, waiting for it to stop. Eventually it did.

Then I noticed something. The distance along the passage appeared longer than the combined size of the two rooms on the right-hand side. I paced off the passage, then paced off the two rooms: the guest bedroom and the darkroom. I was right; the passage was a good two paces longer.

Inside the bedroom I examined the wall adjoining the darkroom. Set square in the centre was a mirror about six feet wide and maybe four feet high. I tried looking behind it but the mounting was tight against the wall and appeared to be a fixture.

In the darkroom, the opposite side of the wall was shelved to take jars of chemicals and packets of printing paper. Even with the light on it wasn't too easy to see in there but eventually I found how it worked. A catch released the shelving which came away from the wall silently and smoothly. Behind was a door. It was locked. I examined it carefully. It wasn't the kind that credit cards open.

I went back into Terita Montez's bedroom and

searched it again. This time I knew what I was looking for. It didn't take long to find. Terita Montez might have imagination for some things but hiding keys wasn't one of them. The key was taped to the underside of a drawer in her dressing table. I eased it away, peeled off the tape and went back into the darkroom. It didn't fit. I went back into the bedroom, slid the drawer right out and held it up above my head. Another key was taped further back. I peeled that one off and returned to the darkroom. This time I'd got it right.

Opening the door I stepped into the tiny room built between the darkroom and the bedroom. The mirror was two-way, something I had already guessed at. Mounted on a tripod in the room was a video camera all encased in material I took to be soundproofing. There was no cassette in the camera and neither were there any cassettes lying around loose. Two recorders stood on a low table.

Reluctantly, because I'd hoped for more than this, I closed up the room, slid the shelving back into place and took the key back into the bedroom. As I did so the telephone began to ring I counted four rings, then it stopped. I waited. It rang again and I picked it up.

'She's on her way back,' Lieutenant Bercovici said.

'Thanks,' I said and hung up.

I replaced the key then stood there, studying the other one. On impulse I went into the adjoining bathroom and ran hot water onto a tablet of soap. Pressing the key into the soap I hoped it would work although I had some doubts. There was lettering and a number of the key which didn't come out too well in the impression so I wrote them down then wrapped the soap in several pieces of Kleenex. I replaced the second key, slid the drawer into place and went swiftly down the stairs.

During my search I'd noticed one or two items that might attract a casual burglar and I picked them up on the way out. I couldn't conceal the fact that a break-in had occurred but I might be able to divert Terita's attention from the obvious.

It had stopped raining and the sky outside was brightening again as I went out onto the patio. I heard a car drive into the front of the house. It couldn't be Terita Montez, not if the lieutenant had called immediately she'd left.

I slid around the corner to the utility room I'd seen earlier. A door opened into it from the poolside and I could see through the window all the way up to the garage. It wasn't the car that had passed me before. For a moment I thought no one was in it but then the door opened and Clara King scrambled down from a special high seat. I waited until she had gone up to the front door of the house, then ran across the garden, dumped the *objets d'art* I'd stolen from the house in the shrubbery and unbolted the garden gate.

Outside I was on the point of crossing to my car when I heard another vehicle coming up the road. Thinking fast, I scrambled through a hedge and found myself in the garden of Helen Jerome's house.

I walked up towards the house, hoping she wouldn't mind an unannounced and unorthodox visit. There was an old-fashioned wrought-iron archway, liberally hung with pink American Pillar roses, which straddled the path. As I walked through the arch I was suddenly aware of someone standing to one side.

As I began to turn something hit me on the back of the head. I started to think, Oh, no, not again. I even started to say it but all that came out was, 'Oh', before I fell forward onto my knees and passed out.

Chapter Seven

I couldn't have been out for more than a split-second because I was still on my knees and Helen Jerome was clucking around me like a mother hen who's just inadvertantly stepped on one of her chicks.

'I'm so sorry, Mr Mace,' she was saying as she helped me to my feet. 'I was a little afraid and I just hit out without waiting to see who you were.'

I shook my head and instantly wished I hadn't. 'That's okay,' I told her, trying for a grin. 'You got me on my hardest spot.'

'Come inside,' she insisted and I didn't need too much encouragement.

We went into the room with all the pictures on the walls. A movie projector was set up with a portable screen propped up across the room.

I let her fuss and mother me into an armchair and rush off to make tea.

'You've caught me indulging myself,' she said when she came back with a tray.

She meant the projector. I picked up a film can and read the label. It was *Countess from Chicago*. 'Very nice,' I said. 'I wish I could watch it with you.'

'I'd like that,' she said.

'Unfortunately . . .'

'. . . not today.' She smiled. 'I understand. Still having problems with my neighbour?'

'Yes.' I glanced around. 'Can I use the phone?'

'Of course. You stay there and drink your tea and I'll bring the phone in here for you.'

I didn't argue although her tea-making wouldn't have won any prizes in Liverpool.

With the phone plugged in, she insisted on topping up my teacup then made to leave.

'Don't go, no secrets from you.'

She smiled and I found myself wishing that time could stand still and she could have stayed the way she had been in her heydays. Then I saw the reels of film stacked beside the projector and realised that in a way time had stopped. For some people, maybe even for her when she watched old films, Helen Jerome always would be young and beautiful.

I called the lieutenant's home but there was no reply. So I called her office. She sounded harassed and from the guarded way she was speaking I guessed she had someone in the room with her.

'Everything okay?' she asked.

'Yes.'

'Get anything?'

'Yes, but I'm not sure what. I take it you're busy.'

'Too damn right I'm busy. We have a panic on.' I could hear her speaking to someone else, then she came back on to me. 'Okay, I'm free for a moment. Listen, we need every man we can lay hands on right now. That means we've had to call the guards off those two girls from The Blue Whale. Can you take a look at them?'

'Give me their addresses.'

I copied down what she told me. 'When can we meet?'

'God knows. Have you anyplace to stay?'

'No.'

'Call me here when you've checked out the girls.'

'Okay,' I said. 'What's the panic about?' I asked but she'd hung up on me before the words were out.

'Trouble?' Helen Jerome asked.

'I'm not sure.' I stood up, looking for someplace to stand my teacup.

She took it from me. 'Those wet clothes will not do,' she said reprovingly.

'I know.'

'Well, see that you change as soon as possible,' she ordered.

'I will,' I assured her.

'And try to find time to come back and we'll watch the film together. In fact, I won't screen the rest of it now. I'll spend the time looking at some other old scraps I have.'

I noticed that she had splicers and other gadgets I wasn't sure about. 'You know how to use all these things?'

'I made it my business to know. Too many of the young people in our business today think all there is to acting is walking on the set and reciting lines. It's a complex business and you can't hope to survive for long if you don't know something about everything.'

I noticed how she didn't think of herself as being out of the business even if she hadn't made a movie for a quarter of a century. Once a movie star, always a movie star I supoose. The same thing happens to coppers.

I went out the way I'd come in, overriding her protests about scrambling through the hedge again. And it was me she was worried about, not the shrubbery.

I drove up onto Ventura, then called into the store where I'd bought my newly ruined clothes. The salesman managed not to ask the questions that were obviously burning on his lips and once more rigged out, I headed for the nearest of the two addresses Lieutenant Bercovici had given me.

By now it was early evening and stores were closing, the traffic thickening as some people went home and others made an early start to Saturday night.

The first of the addresses was for the girl I knew nothing about. Her name was Carol White and she lived over in Boyle Heights. The house was better than I'd expected, part of a recent development. I rang the bell and waited.

A figure appeared at the other side of the door, silhouetted through the hammered glass panel. 'Who is it?' a voice asked. It was a man.

I told him my name and that I wanted to see Carol and that I was a friend of Lieutenant Bercovici and if he wanted to check that was okay with me.

He went away and I stood there, listening to the hum of a vacuum cleaner next door. It was almost peaceful although that could have been caused by the fact that just across the way was a large cemetery.

After several minutes the man came back and I heard two bolts being shot and a lock turned. A face peered out, weighed me up and then disappeared again as he closed the door to release the safety chain.

I went in and the man backed off down the corridor, never taking his eyes off me. We ended up in a small cluttered room. Now I could see the man. He was young, maybe twenty-four, and had the build of a body-builder who'd stopped training. A lot of muscles but coated in unhealthy fat. He stepped aside and a girl peeped out from behind him. She was younger than Muscles and pretty in an ordinary, mousey-brown way.

'Carol?' I asked.

She nodded.

I asked her if she could tell me anything about Linda and where she might have gone to hide.

'I don't really know her,' she said. 'Ella knew her best.' Her face puckered. 'Poor Ella.'

'Yes,' I said. 'Poor Ella.'

'What's all this about?' Muscles asked.

'It's complicated.'

'Is Carol in danger?'

'I don't know,' I admitted.

'First the cops put a guard outside, then they take him away again. What the hell's going on?'

'Like I said, it's complicated. Look, can you stay here until we can get the guard replaced?'

'Sure.'

'And don't let anyone in unless you clear it personally with either Lieutenant Bercovici or me.' I thought about Officers Mullany and Carling. 'Not even if it's a cop,' I added.

'Okay,' he said.

I turned back to Carol. 'There's nothing you can think of that might help me find Linda?'

She shook her head. 'I haven't been in for a week. I've been sick.'

I smiled cheerfully, trying to give her confidence even I didn't feel. 'Keep thinking about it,' I said. 'I'll call you later and see if anything's come back.'

I went out and back along the passageway. Muscles followed me. 'Have you got a gun?' I asked quietly.

'No. Shit, this is bad isn't it.'

'Maybe. Just stay alert. You live here?'

'We're getting married next month.' He wasn't sounding too sure.

He let me out and I stood on the step listening to him slide the bolts and chain and turn the key in the lock. I hoped it would be enough.

I drove around the cemetery, then swung south through Vernon then headed west until Crenshaw. The other girl lived on 48th Street and I rang the bell alongside her made up name of Michelle LaRue on the door of a high, timber-fronted house that looked in bad need of maintenance.

No one came to the door, no one spoke to me from the little grille beside the name board. I tried the door but it was locked. I rang bells until someone spoke to me. I said I was a police officer which was true even if I wasn't what the voice would assume me to be. A few moments later a middle-aged frowsy woman stood in the doorway.

'She has the room at the back but she went out.'

'When?'

'Right after the cop took off. What's going on?'

I ignored the question and went down to the door she indicated. The name was repeated on the door. Michelle LaRue. Where did they get them from? I leaned on the door until it opened with a splintering protest. The frowsy woman didn't complain. Maybe she'd met my kind of policeman before. The apartment was shabby and empty.

'Any idea where she might have gone?' I asked.

She shrugged. 'Who the hell knows where these kids go.' She ran her eyes over me from head to toe and back again. 'How about a drink?'

I shook my head. 'Maybe another time.'

She sighed. 'That's what they all say.'

I grinned and went out into the street. I scribbled the lieutenant's telephone number on a piece of paper. 'If she comes back, have her call this number. It's very important, tell her.'

She took the paper, pushing it suggestively down the front of a none-too-clean sweater.

Back in the car I sat for a few minutes, uneasily aware that I didn't know where next to turn. I was no closer to finding Linda than I'd ever been. All I did have was a collection of miscellaneous pieces of information none of which added up. It was unsettling, knowing that someone, somewhere, was very probably looking for Linda at this moment with something decidedly unpleasant on his mind.

If I didn't get anywhere soon I would have to fall back on the last resort of a good detective, that certain something which all too often was the first resort of a bad copper. I would have to start leaning on people.

Because I wasn't far away and for want of doing something, anything, I drove up to The Blue Whale. It was closed. I sat outside, thinking about that. Twice now the place had been shut. I wondered why. While I was wondering why a car drove up and parked and a very fat man clambered out. Roccisano. I smiled to myself. However good a copper is, sooner or later he needs luck on his side, or coincidence. I'd got both in one fat package.

I waited until he unlocked the door then went across the street at a fast run before he had time to close the door again. I hit the door hard without breaking step and was inside and all over him before he had a chance to find his gun.

Fat or not he was tough and by his sheer bulk he was a hard man to hold. Once he had a knee in my stomach but then tried pulling something from his coat pocket. I grabbed for his arm and yanked, pulling hand and gun out along with a chunk of his coat. I smashed his gun hand on the floor until he let go, then managed to kick the weapon out of reach.

I swung a haymaker into his huge waistline but his fat absorbed all the power. Now he had a stubby-fingered hand across my face, trying to jab my eyes. I bit his thumb. It tasted of garlic. He yelled. I stepped back and let go with a straight right-hand jab to his face. He yelped this time and blood spurted from his nose. Both hands came up to his face and he stood there, an unprotected target. I abandoned any vestiges of sportsmanship and kicked him in the groin, very hard.

He went down, a high-pitched squeal coming from him. He rocked about on his stomach, blood smearing the floor.

I went across to the door and looked out. No one seemed to have heard us. I closed the door, locked it using the keys that he'd dropped when I'd entered, then searched for the light switch.

I helped myself to whiskey from behind the bar, then pulled a chair across to where Roccisano was lying. He was still rocking on his immense stomach but the squealing had changed to a moan. Eventually he pulled himself up onto his knees and stared at me from behind a mask of blood. I walked across and stamped on one of his hands. He screamed. I stamped on the other hand and the scream stopped as abruptly as it had begun. Behind the blood his face went dark. For a moment I thought I'd gone too far and he was having a heart attack. Then his face changed colour again and he shook his head painfully from side to side.

'Okay,' I said. 'Suppose you tell me what all this is about.'

He tried levering himself upright but I reached out and pushed him back down again. I walked across to find his gun and brought it back and cocked it, pointing it carefully at his legs.

'How about a kneecap?' I asked.

'For Chrissake, you sonofabitch.'

'Talk,' I said.

'What do you want to know?'

'Everything.'

'For Chrissake . . .'

'Okay, let's start with who killed Ella?'

'I don't know,' he said quickly. Too quickly.

I moved the gun until the muzzle rested on his left knee.

'I don't know,' he yelled.

'Okay, where's Linda?'

'I don't know.'

'Where's the bartender from this place?'

'I don't know.'

'That's the fourth time you've said that. It's becoming boring.'

'Then try asking me something I do know.'

He was sounding more confident now. I wondered why my questions weren't alarming him. Maybe I was on the wrong track. If that was so, then I was in worse shape than I'd thought.

'What were you doing at Terita Montez's house the day I saw you there?'

'Collecting.'

'What?'

'Films, what else?'

'How did you get out of the pool?'

He didn't answer and I jabbed him with the gun. 'Those two cops, they pulled me out.'

'Why?'

'Why? What do you mean, why? I woulda drowned, that's why.'

'Why should they care?'

He thought about that for a moment, until I jabbed him again.

'Terry told 'em to.'

'Do they always do as she tells them?'

'How would I know.' He saw my hand move. 'Okay, okay. I guess she pays for a few privileges.'

'Another of the girls who works here, Michelle LaRue, real name Barbara Collis. Where can I find her?'

He thought for a moment. 'She lives just off Crenshaw, 46th, 48th Street, one of those.'

'And if she isn't there?'

He thought again, something in his piggy eyes gleaming disturbingly. 'She has a brother, lives over in Lennox just behind the airport. I forget his name.'

'Then try remembering.'

He made another effort. 'Larry, no, Leo. That's it, Leo Collis. Black dude, about thirty, thinks he's a real hard nut.'

'Like you?'

'You bastard, Mace.'

'Where does this Collis hang out?

'I don't know.'

I raised the gun towards his groin.

'I don't for Chrissake. Look, there's a pool-hall on 111th, you could try there.'

I thought about this for a moment. He might be telling me the truth, then again he might not. Either way, there was only one way to prove it. 'Okay, get up,' I said. 'Let's go visiting.'

He scrambled to his feet.

I went behind the bar and filled a bowl with water. 'Wash the blood off your face,' I told him.

Outside I relocked the door of The Blue Whale and prodded Roccisano across the street to my car. I made him get in the back seat, facing backwards. He could barely make it but once he was jammed in there any move he made would be telegraphed.

I drove away, taking directions from the fat man. At

a set of lights a car drew up alongside and a pretty blonde girl looked across at me and smiled. I smiled back but then her eyes shifted to a point behind me and the smile faded. I grinned and shrugged my shoulders at her. She still looked puzzled but she'd seen nothing to call a cop about.

The lights changed and I moved off, realising I was crossing Manchester Avenue. Seeing the name made me think about just how far away from home I was.

When we reached 111th Street I drove along it until the pool-hall came in sight. I drove straight on past hearing Roccisano sigh in what could have been relief. It made me uneasy. I picked up signs to the parking area at LAX and drove there. The entry gate was operated automatically and no one was idle enough to look in the back of my car. Everyone seemed to have someplace to go and something to do. I found a relatively quiet corner and stopped.

'Take your trousers off,' I told the fat man.

'What?'

I showed him the gun and he did as he was told. It was a real struggle but he made it in the end. I took them from him. 'Okay, get out.'

He stared hard at me, I guess he was thinking which way he would kill me if the opportunity ever arose. Then he clambered out and stood there in his underpants. I put the car in gear and drove away. I checked in the rearview mirror. He hadn't moved. I reckoned his brain would be too occupied with how to get out of there without being arrested to allow his feet to function as well.

I paid the parking toll and as I drove back along 111th I dropped the fat man's trousers from the window. I had his gun, that was all I needed for a memento.

The pool-hall was brightly-lit with green and red neon. I parked the car, noticing there were not many white people about.

The neon told me the place was called the Eight Ball, which didn't show a lot of imagination but when I got inside there were no white people at all. Maybe the sign had more meaning than I'd thought. It crossed my mind that Roccisano might have sent me in somewhere that could spell trouble. Maybe that was why he'd sighed when we drove straight on past. If he had set me up, it was too late to do anything about it.

An old man sat behind a table just inside the door. He looked at me warily out of a face that had all the charm and grace of a tightly clenched fist. I told him I was looking for a man named Leo Collis.

He studied me in silence for several long seconds, then glanced across the room and moved his head fractionally. I looked up to see every pair of eyes in the place were on me. I was glad I had Roccisano's gun.

We had similar places back home; snooker halls had been popular way back, then had faded and all-but died. Thanks to TV and millions being made out of the game the halls were suddenly popular again and almost respectable. They were still a good hideout for small-time villains and other layabouts but mostly they were somewhere to go for the unemployed and hopeful TV snooker stars of the future.

I had a feeling that the Eight Ball had a higher proportion of villains than any counterpart in Liverpool. I was suddenly acutely aware that I was a long way from home and this was the kind of joint where coppers go in twos only when there aren't more of them.

A thin, bespectacled youth came across the room, weaving through the suddenly disused pool tables. I recalled the way Lieutenant Bercovici had threaded her way through the tables in the Hollywood restaurant. The youth had almost as much sinuosity but ten times as much threat. He didn't take his eyes off me as he approached.

'Man here wants Leo,' the old man said.

'Who're you?' the youth asked.

I told him my name.

'Cop?'

I thought about how I should answer. This didn't seem like a good place to be caught telling lies. 'Not in this town,' I said.

He too studied me for a while, then turned and went back the way he had come. By now my eyes were growing accustomed to the dim lighting. The low-slung lamps over the tables kept in dark shadow anyone who stood upright. At the moment everyone was doing exactly that.

The youth reached the table where he had been playing with a man in a fancy white suit. After a moment the man in white carefully leaned over and lined up a shot. He had a lot of gold on his fingers. He potted the ball neatly. Without changing his position he glanced across at me, his eyes gleaming with multicoloured reflected light.

I looked at him unblinkingly. Then he rested his cue against the table, straightened up and came over to me. As if some hidden movie director had suddenly yelled 'action' the room came to life, games resumed, talk started up, laughter echoed and bottles and glasses clinked.

The man in the white suit was handsome in a studied manner. He looked as though he spent a lot of time in front of a mirror deciding what to wear and what expressions to choose to go with his clothes. His hair was neat, almost straight.

'Leo Collis?' I asked.

He inclined his head.

I told him my name.
'Where you from?' he asked.
Once again there was no point in lying. 'I'm from England. Over there I'm a police officer. Over here, I'm not.'
'Okay, Mr Mace from England, what you want?'
'I'm looking for a girl named Linda Martin. She's English too. She works at The Blue Whale on Coliseum Street.'
Collis's face closed, his eyes watchful.
'Two of the girls from the same place have been killed. Ella, called herself Francoise, and Maria the Mexican girl.'
His expression changed. I'd told him something he didn't already know.
'Two other girls from The Blue Whale might be in danger. The LAPD put guards on them, now they've taken the guards off. The two girls are Carol White and your sister. Carol's got protection, I don't know about Barbara. She's left her home on 48th Street.'
He thought over what I'd said. 'If the cops have called off the guard, then maybe there's no more danger.'
'I don't think so,' I said.
'This danger you think Barbara's in, how bad is it, Mr English Mace?'
'I think someone wants information bad enough to torture her, maybe even kill her. That's what happened to Maria. Someone cut her breasts off and she bled to death.'
His eyes widened and some of his studied impassivity faded. 'Shiiit. So that's why they closed the joint down.'
I guessed he was talking about the barroom. 'So, do you know where Barbara is now?'

'I could maybe guess.'

I leaned forward and changed the tone of my voice. 'Then I suggest you do exactly that, Mr Collis because otherwise Barbara could be in very serious trouble.'

'Okay, okay. I'll go see her and tell her to keep out of sight.'

I shook my head. 'Not good enough. For one thing, the guy looking for her might be smarter than either of us; for another, I want to ask her some questions.'

He gave this some thought, then nodded slowly. 'Okay, let's take a little drive.'

I turned and let him follow me out into the street. Leo Collis wasn't the kind of man I would normally turn my back on but these seemed like exceptional circumstances. I led the way to my car and unlocked it.

He glanced at me across the roof. 'You carrying?' he asked.

I nodded.

'Okay,' he said and climbed in.

Once again that night I took directions and we were soon heading east on Imperial. I pulled a mental picture of my already well-thumbed street plan from my mind. I was heading towards Watts which awoke recollections of race riots twenty years back. I hoped relations had improved.

'You come all the way from England just to find this Linda?' Collis asked.

I thought that was worth a small lie. 'Yes,' I told him.

'Must be pretty important.'

I could tell from his voice how his mind was working. 'Her father is a friend of mine. A good friend. Nobody gets paid for any of this, Leo. All we get out of tonight is that maybe we save your sister's life. You want to put a price on that?'

He lapsed into silence, broken only by monosyllabic directions.

We crossed Central Avenue without a sign of a breakdown and after a few more twists and turns he told me to pull over to the curb and stop.

'Barbara called me earlier,' Collis said. 'Said she needed a place to stay. She didn't say nothing about no killings. I told her to come here.' He sounded very casual about it all.

'You didn't think to come over and see what the trouble was?'

'She didn't say she was in trouble. Anyway, what's it to you, man?'

I shook my head. 'Nothing. Man. Let's go.'

'You go the rest of the way alone,' he said. 'You're carrying and I'm not.'

'It's because I'm carrying that you come with me.'

He frowned. 'Why?'

I tapped Roccisano's gun where it lay in my pocket. 'Because I've got the power.'

He looked at me curiously, as if wondering whether or not I would use the gun. He must have known that I wouldn't but he almost grinned and got out of the car. I locked the car door securely, uncomfortably aware that most people around here probably could open up the car and have it away in less time that it would take me to open the door of the building we were outside.

It was a hotel although it was impossible to tell until we were inside. No sign proclaimed it as such but there was a desk and a rack of pigeon holes with keys. A tattered chart on the wall gave the rates by the hour and by the night. People didn't stay here longer than that.

Collis reached over the desk and took a key from pigeon hole eleven. We went up the stairs, him leading until we were on the third floor. He handed me the key and pointed to the door of number thirty-one.

I suppose having keys that worked on all floors made life easier, especially for anyone working the badger game.

I put my ear to the door and listened, uncomfortably aware that my record so far on visiting the young dancers from The Blue Whale wasn't a good one. Two dead, one missing and one scared out of her wits.

I tapped gently. Nothing.

'Barbara,' I called softly. 'I'm a friend, don't be afraid. I've got Leo out here with me.' I gestured at him.

Cautiously, he came closer. 'Barbara, honey. It's okay. This guy's almost a brother.'

I suppose that was as close to a compliment as he had been for a long time.

From inside the room I heard a sound, then a bolt was pulled back, then a key turned in the lock. I was meeting more than my share of frightened people tonight.

The girl who stood there when the door finally opened was tiny, her huge eyes making her face seem even smaller than it was. She was light-skinned but not enough to pass, even if she'd wanted to. These days it wasn't supposed to be necessary but I suppose circumstances alter cases. Any way out of the life she must lead would be worth trying.

She glanced down and a hand leaped to her mouth. I realised I was holding Roccisano's gun. I hadn't even known I'd taken it out. I put the gun away and she moved aside to let us in.

The room was seedy and dirty. A bed and a chair was all that served as furniture. The blind was pulled down but a tear in it allowed light through from the street lamps. A single bulb, covered in a handmade fold of paper threw a harsh-angled light down onto the bed.

Barbara was wearing a blue dress that gleamed in the light. Satin, maybe.

I went across to the chair and sat down. After a moment, eyes watchful, she sat on the bed, her posture making her look like a frightened animal about to dart off into the safety of the undergrowth.

'What's happening?' she asked Collis.

He shrugged his shoulders and looked at me.

'Do you know what's happened to Ella and Maria?' I asked.

Her head bobbed. 'The cops said Ella was dead. What's happened to Maria?'

'Maria's been killed too,' I said quietly. Apart from stiffening slightly she didn't respond. She'd probably worked that much out for herself and all I was doing was confirming a suspicion.

'I think it's all something to do with what Linda and Ella did on Monday night,' I went on.

She thought about that for a moment. 'I wasn't working Monday,' she said.

'I know. I was at The Blue Whale myself.'

'So how can I be mixed up in this?'

'Linda is missing. Someone wants to find her very badly. So badly they killed Maria because she didn't tell them anything. Couldn't tell them anything.'

'They cut her tits off,' Collis said.

I glared up at him. Barbara's eyes went from me to him and back again, her hands involuntarily clutching at her own tiny, pointed breasts.

'Can you tell me anything at all,' I said. 'Anything that will help me find Linda before they do.'

She was trying to think but panic was setting in. Collis had helped that along with his contribution. She shook her head.

'Okay,' I said. 'If you think of anything, well, you will tell me won't you?'

She nodded, birdlike and anxious.

'Right now, I think you should find someplace else to hide out. If I found you this easy then others might.'

'How did you do it?' Collis asked.

'A man told me your name, a fat man.'

'Roccisano?' the girl asked.

'Yes.'

She looked worried. It was contagious. I was worried. If Roccisano had sorted out the problem of being without trousers he might be setting something in motion right now. I didn't know if he had friends.

'Where can I go?' Barbara asked.

I didn't know but I had to say something. 'Come with me,' I told her. 'I'll find somewhere for you.'

Slowly, reluctant to leave even the tiny hotel room, she picked up a thin coat that lay crumpled on the floor and put it on.

I opened the door and checked the landing, then we went down the stairs. I led, Collis came last. He'd slipped on some dark glasses which made the ill-lit stairwell a hazard but maybe he thought they also made him invisible.

In the street more people were about than when we'd gone into the hotel. No one appeared to pay any attention to us.

I unlocked the car and gestured to Collis and Barbara to come out of the hotel.

They were almost at the car when the shooting started.

Chapter Eight

There were two shots, spaced. It was the space that saved me.

The first shot was high, right over my head. The rolling echo from the gun across the street blended with the crack as the bullet hit the wall of the hotel. I did three things at once. I reached for Roccisano's gun, I grabbed Barbara Collis by the arm, and I went down, fast, behind the car. The second bullet went through the airspace I'd just vacated.

I yanked open the car door and almost threw the girl inside.

People were shouting. Close by, a woman's voice rose in a high-pitched wail of fear.

I rolled to one side until I was by the front wheel of the car and snapped off a shot in the general direction of where I thought the gunmen were.

Turning my head I saw Leo Collis was crouched in the hotel doorway, a green neon sign, flashing on and off, was lighting up his smart white suit like a Christmas tree.

'Get in the car,' I yelled at him.

He came out of the doorway, crablike, scuttling across towards me. I saw he had a gun in his hand. He'd been armed all along. Then he changed direction, started along the street, paused and fired into the shadows.

There was an answering blast of gunfire but I was busy scrambling into the car after the girl. I fumbled the keys, then got the engine started. There was another shot; something hit the side of the car like a giant fist. The girl was whimpering in fright.

The spacing and sound of the shots had told me there were at least two gunmen, with different calibre weapons. It seemed entirely academic.

The car was rolling now. I still had the door open. I could see Leo Collis. He was slumped against the wall. The green flashing light wasn't the only thing discolouring his suit. A huge red stain was forming on the once-immaculate chest. I looked at his face. His dark glasses were tilted to one side. A bullet had gone clear through one lens and into his eye. Blood poured down his face.

I hit the accelerator and the car surged forward. I didn't hear more shots but the rear window exploded inwards showering debris over me and the girl.

'Leo, where's Leo?' Barbara was trying to scamble upright.

I reached out a hand and pushed her savagely back down again.

'Leo!' she cried.

This was no time to do things the way policemen are taught. 'He's dead,' I yelled. 'Now stay down.'

I tried working out where I was and where I was headed but I'd driven the first couple of hundred yards without conscious thought. I didn't even know if I'd turned any corners.

The street I was in was narrow, lined both sides with parked cars. It was well-lit, lots of people about walking and talking and looking as though they were having fun. Someone wandered into the street ahead of me. Local custom favours pedestrians over motorists. It didn't then. I hit the horn and the man jumped a foot in the air and came down running. As I went past I heard a yell of anger.

I risked a look in the rear-view mirror. He was back in the middle of the street again, waving his arms at me. Then I saw another set of car headlights silhouette the man for a split-second before he leaped to safety again. I knew that we had company.

I made a fast left turn, tyres squealing the way they do in the movies, then tried a right with the same accompanying sound effects. I also had the same accompanying car. And it was gaining.

Now I was in a long road that stretched far ahead of me in an unbroken straight line, well-lit all the way with a scattering of traffic signals. I pushed the throttle hard down and really wound the car up to its maximum. But I wasn't shaking the other vehicle. I wasn't about to lose it on the straight so it was back to alley driving.

At the first set of traffic lights, which were at red, I made a right turn, sneaking through under the wheels of a truck that lurched sideways, a sound like an ocean-going liner in fog bellowing irately at me.

I risked a study of the overhanging street signs. I was on Alameda Street and it was dual carriageway and too well lit for comfort. An upcoming turning was into Century Boulevard so I made that and almost at once made another left which sent me back in the opposite direction along a much narrower and darker street lined with apartment houses.

I slowed down, watching the mirror. Nothing followed. I turned right, then left, then right again. Still nothing.

I drove steadily for some moments down a long street then saw the lights of a main road crossing ahead. I turned left onto it, noting I was on Atlantic Avenue. I still didn't know towards which point of the compass I was heading.

My pulse rate was slowing and I reached down to help the girl onto the seat. At that instant the car lurched forward as something hit the back end with a metallic bang.

I glanced over my shoulder, thinking another car had rammed us but the nearest vehicle was twenty yards back. Then the bang came again. Someone in the other car was shooting at us; somehow they'd caught up with us again.

I pushed the hire car to its limits yet again but the other was gaining. It began to overhaul us and in desperation I twitched the wheel, causing my back end to crack into their front wing. They fell back, then came again. Once more I tried the same routine. It worked but I knew it was only a matter of time.

Then, suddenly, there were more lights behind, flashing lights, and the undulating howl of a police siren.

Ahead I could see a cluster of lights rising and falling in swinging arcs. A major intersection. Almost side by side with the pursuing car I crouched low over the wheel urging more speed by will power.

I risked a sideways glance. I saw a flash of white on black. The gunman with the afro who'd tried to kill me at the mental hospital had a bandage around his head, holding his jaw in place. Then I saw the gun in his hand and dropped my head.

A splintering crack told me he'd fired, the bullet coming in my side window and going straight out the other side.

Then his car surged ahead, taking him out of position for another try. Now I was the pursuer but the police car was gaining.

Then we were at the intersection. The car ahead went one way, I went another. We both had the same idea though. Round and round the intersection we went, up and down, under and over a freeway.

The patrol car joined the same crazy switchback and at one point we were all together within a few feet of one another, except I was going one way on one road, the police were below me going the same way and the gunmen's car travelling in the opposite direction above me.

Then the patrol car was on the tail of the gunmen and both cars went off the intersection and down onto the freeway. I twisted the wheel, dived off onto the road we'd come along and started back towards Watts. Not far though. As soon as I saw a side turning I went down it like a rat up a drainpipe.

I stopped, turned off the engine and killed the lights. I could hear police sirens wailing in all directions. Half the LAPD must be out on the trail. I knew there was a chance the patrol car would have my licence number and have radioed it to everyone else in the hunt. Keeping this car wasn't smart. Tonight's events would take some explaining.

Along from where I was parked was a small flatbed truck. I hopped out, tried the truck door and it opened. Fumbling under the dash I found a bunch of wires and in the light from nearby street lamps I managed to figure out which were what. As the truck's engine leaped into life I yelled for Barbara. She didn't come so I ran back to the car and pulled her out, almost carrying her to the truck.

Moments later we were driving sedately along, with

nothing more to worry about; except that I'd added theft of a motor vehicle to what was now an alarmingly escalating list of arrestable offences.

I decided that the best move now was somewhere to stay for the remaining hours of the night and as I didn't relish driving far in a stolen truck I kept an eye out for a hotel or motel. Calmer by now, I was able to take in that we were back in Vernon. We couldn't be too far from Barbara's home but that didn't seem like a bright idea.

'Are there any hotels around here?' I asked. 'Places where not too many questions are asked?'

She didn't reply.

I shook her hard. This was no time for being kind and sympathetic. 'Snap out of it, Barbara. Hotels. Do you know any?'

She shook herself free of my grip, peering through the windscreen. 'Turn right,' she said.

I did as I was told.

'There,' she pointed.

The hotel looked like a twin of the one she'd been in when Leo and I had found her but at least it boasted a sign outside. Calling a dump like this The Commodore showed a fine sense of optimism.

I pulled over to the curb and went in.

A clerk dozed behind a scarred counter. As I walked over to him one eye opened. 'Twenty,' he said without moving his lips.

I didn't argue. I gave him the twenty and without rising out of his seat he reached for a key and handed it across.

'Go back to sleep,' I said.

He looked at me.

'Sleep,' I repeated.

Light dawned and he settled back, closing his eyes again.

I brought Barbara in, taking her quickly past the clerk

and up the stairs. If this place had ever been painted it was long enough ago for all signs to have worn away revealing only flaking plaster and crumbling brickwork. Only force of habit kept the place upright.

The room was as bad as the stairs and passageways suggested it might be. Twin beds, an unpainted wooden cupboard that I presumed served as a wardrobe, a cracked washbasin with a dripping tap, a ratty old chair and a square of carpet so threadbare it was impossible to see what the colour and pattern had been.

I turned off the unshaded ceiling light, went across to the window and looked out. The street was quiet. I opened the window to let some of the stale air out and after pulling down the shade I turned on a wobbly bedside lamp.

'I'll be about twenty minutes,' I told Barbara.

'You're going?' Her voice went up the scale.

'I have to ditch the truck away from here. I won't be long. Don't open the door. Right?'

She nodded.

I went to the door and glanced along the passage. Three doors away was a bathroom. 'Do you need the bathroom?' I asked.

She needed to think about it but eventually nodded again.

'Go now,' I told her.

I waited until she was back, then went out, waited for her to turn the key in the lock and went downstairs.

The clerk hadn't moved.

'Any all-night stores around here?' I asked.

'What kind?' He didn't open his eyes. Twenty bucks seemed to be buying a fair amount of discretion.

'Food.'

'Two blocks east.'

'Which is east?'

He opened an eye. 'Turn right as you go out.'

I leaned over the counter and put my face an inch from his. His cheeks were pitted with the scars of childhood acne. He was about forty, his breath carried the sour smell of cheap booze. 'Don't move out of that chair until I get back,' I said.

'Huh?'

'Stay put.'

'Suppose I want to go to the can?'

'Then pee in your pants,' I told him.

'You're kidding.'

'You'll prefer it to the alternative,' I assured him.

He shrugged his shoulders and closed his eyes again.

I went out, climbed in the truck, started up the engine with the wires again and drove past the all-night store until I found a payphone.

I reached Lieutenant Bercovici at her office. She sounded bad tempered.

'Trouble,' I said. 'I've got the Collis girl with me and I think we'll be okay tonight but I'm not happy about Carol. Can you put the guard back?'

'I'll try but I doubt it. We have the makings of a race riot on our hands. Some white men shot up a hotel in Watts and killed a black guy . . . Oh, God. His name was Collis. Are you . . .'

'I'll tell you later,' I said hastily.

'Mace . . .'

'Later. Look, can you pick me up. I've had to ditch the car.'

'Not right now.'

'Okay, we'll survive the night I expect. Can I bring her to your place tomorrow morning?'

There was the briefest of pauses. 'Okay. About Collis . . .'

I hung up.

I dialled again and heard a muffled male voice answer. I guessed it was Muscles. 'This is Mace. Everything okay?'

'Yeah.'

'I'm trying to get the cop back on watch but it won't be tonight.'

'That's okay, some of the guys came around. Anyone tries anything here and they'll be in trouble.'

I hoped he was right but an uncomfortable image of Leo Collis floated into my mind.

I left the truck beside the payphone and walked back to the store. I bought a bag of barbecued chicken legs, some bread and a six-pack. As an afterthought I added a couple of cans of Pepsi and a bottle of milk.

I didn't pass anyone as I walked down the street to The Commodore. I could hear police sirens wailing faintly in the night air. I hoped the lieutenant had been exaggerating. A race riot was the last thing I wanted on my conscience.

The desk clerk hadn't moved. I didn't remember seeing soap and towels in the room so I asked him for both. His expression suggested this was among the most unusual requests he'd ever had. He managed to find a towel, almost clean but soap was something he didn't have.

I went upstairs, rapped softly on the room door and whispered my name. Barbara let me in.

She had taken off her shoes and was even tinier. Frail and helpless, she stood there, looking up at me. Tears formed in her eyes but didn't roll down her cheeks.

I dumped my purchases on one of the beds and put my arms around her and let her cry.

After a while she pulled away and went to sit on the

other bed. I made an attempt to get her to eat something but she wasn't interested in food.

I found the piece of soap I'd used to make an impression of the key hidden in Terita Montez's bedroom. I used my nailfile to slice off a piece. The way things were going this nailfile would soon qualify for a place in the Policeman's Hall of Fame. I washed my face and hands, then persuaded Barbara to do the same.

'I'm sorry about your brother,' I said, when she was back sitting on the other bed again.

She nodded without speaking.

'Tomorrow, I'll find someplace safe for you to stay until all this is over.'

'Thank you,' she said, her voice small and far off.

I took a chicken leg out of the bag, broke off a piece of bread and persuaded her to eat.

'I didn't see much of Leo,' she said after a while, her words muffled by a mouthful of food. 'We didn't have any folks. They died. He drifted away. I stayed with my aunt. Then she died. I got work dancing.' I was getting a life history, in short, sad sentences. I let her speak. Maybe it would help her. 'I did okay. Even did a TV show once. Then I got pregnant. I lost it. That's when I started working for Mr Corelli.'

'Corelli?'

'Owns The Blue Whale. Works the bar. Looks like a fighter.'

The bartender had told me some fancy tale about the bar's owner living in luxury someplace else. Maybe Barbara had got it wrong.

'Why did they kill Ella and Maria?' she asked suddenly.

'I think it's because Ella and Linda saw something.'

She nodded her head, remembering what I'd told her at the other hotel. Her hands clasped her small breasts in the same gesture she'd made before. 'Did they really cut . . .?'

I nodded.

She didn't want any more of the chicken and I took it from her, dropped it into the bag, then wiped her fingers on the towel. She sat there, letting me look after her like a father.

'Try to get some sleep,' I said.

She nodded, then stood up and unselfconsciously stepped out of her blue satin dress. All she was wearing beneath was a pair of matching blue briefs little bigger than the g-string the girls at The Blue Whale wore. I looked away, guilty at feeling lust for her at such a time.

When I looked back the briefs were on the floor with the dress and she was in the other bed.

I picked up dress and underwear and laid them neatly on the arm of the old chair. Then I sat on my bed, thinking. After a while I undressed down to my underpants and turned out the light before sliding between the sheets.

I recalled the sequence of shots before Leo Collis was killed. Two shots, one just over my head, another that would have gone right through me if I hadn't hit the deck. Maybe I'd just been the clearest target but I had a feeling that they'd been aimed at me. If Afro had wanted to kill me at the Meridian asylum there was no reason for him to have changed his mind. I was a danger to him, or whoever had hired him. Maybe they'd started out looking for Linda by way of any of the girls who might have clues to her whereabouts but now I was their number two interest. That might mean that Barbara and Carol were no longer in too much danger. I couldn't take risks, of course, not with young and comparatively innocent lives but I came to the conclusion that for now I should take care of me.

But I didn't know why I was the target. I didn't know anything.

I don't know how long I'd lain there but suddenly Barbara was standing beside my bed and lifting the sheet. She slid in beside me, pushing her soft, warm, tiny brown body close to mine.

I tried telling myself that all she wanted was to be close to someone. After a while her breathing told me that really was all that she wanted. She was fast asleep.

I put a cautious arm around her, feeling her breath on my chest. One of her legs curled over mine and she began to stroke my body. Now I didn't know whether she was asleep or awake. I ran a hand down her back, cupping it around her small, firm buttocks. I had a mental image of Linda, felt again the embarrassed guilt of seeing her naked. This girl was about the same age and just as alone if not in quite so much danger. I didn't feel guilt, and I didn't feel embarrassed. There was only one thing I felt. Her hand ran down my body and she felt it too.

Then she moved her head, bringing her lips close to mine. 'Thank you,' she whispered. 'You saved my life.'

I realised that all she had to say thanks with was her body. Reaching down, I took her hand away from me. 'That's okay,' I told her. 'All part of the service.'

'Don't you want to . . ?'

'Let's get some sleep,' I said, not meaning a word of it. 'There's always tomorrow.'

She let out a tiny sigh which might have been relief.

A long time later her breathing told me that this time she really was asleep.

Daylight was pushing its way through the blind long before I could close my eyes and rest.

Chapter Nine

We took a cab from The Commodore all the way across town to Pandora Avenue, or to be precise to the junction of Pico and Glen. I paid off the cab there just in case, and waited until the driver was out of sight before setting out to walk the rest of the way to Lieutenant Bercovici's house.

She must have been watching out for us because the door opened as we came up the path between the geraniums.

The lieutenant didn't say anything to me, giving most of her attention to Barbara. They disappeared up the stairs and when the lieutenant was back I was in the kitchen frying eggs.

'What the hell do you think you're doing?' she demanded.

'I'm hungry. How's Barbara?'

'Taking a bath.' She glared at me. 'Do you mind telling me what's going on?'

I told here about the shooting and how I'd been sent up to Leo by Roccisano.

She was still glaring.

'Has everything calmed down?' I asked.

She nodded as if reluctant to concede that my behaviour hadn't started a race war.

'So what's the problem?' I asked.

'The problem is that you are a visitor, you have no rights, no authority, no nothing. So far you've found two corpses, beaten up and half-drowned a man, you've burgled a house, a film studio, a bar, you've stolen a truck, been chased though the streets by gunmen and a prowl car, a man has been shot to death which almost kicked off another riot that wasn't helped because eye-witnesses thought that you, a white man, were kidnapping Barbara, a black girl.'

She paused for breath. I turned the eggs over in the pan.

'You've forgotten that another girl is missing,' I said. 'The one that started all this off. To say nothing of the fact that the way I'm going I'll soon have trouble hiring a car in this town.' I thought guiltily about the latest rental car, lying in a side street somewhere with bulletholes all over it and half the windows shot out.

'It's no joke, Mace.'

I looked at her set face. She was wearing a lemon yellow chunky sweater today, tucked into soft cord denims the colour of a good malt whiskey. Her slender feet were perched on top of thick wood-soled sandals. I leaned over and kissed the tip of her nose. She pulled her head away.

'Okay, I'm sorry,' I told her. 'I didn't do any of this on purpose. It just sort of happened.'

'And does this kind of thing just sort of happen around Liverpool?'

I shook my head.

'So why does it happen here?'

'I seem to remember you telling me that you had a lot more crime here, all I'm doing is finding evidence that you're right.'

She wasn't amused.

'I'm sorry,' I said again. 'I really didn't start any of it.'

'Maybe not but you're going the right way to finish it.'
'If I knew what "it" was.'
'Those eggs are burning,' she said.
I spooned them out onto a plate. 'Does Barbara want to eat?' I asked.
'Did you have to sleep with her,' she demanded.
I looked at her in silence for a moment, then stood the plate and the pan down and put my arms around her. 'Is that what all this heavy stuff is about? I didn't sleep with her, not in that way. We shared a room because she was in danger. We shared a bed because she was a frightened girl, alone, and she'd just seen her brother shot to death and been almost killed herself. Nothing happened.'
She looked up at me. 'Really?'
I nodded. 'What did she say to you?'
I felt her shrug. 'Just that you'd looked after her and that you'd been kind. She told me she'd spent the night in your bed as if it was something to be proud of.'
I grinned. 'Sounds just like one of my usual conquests.'
'Damn you, Mace . . .'
She was planning on saying more but I stopped her by placing my lips over her mouth. All the frustrated excitement of last night came back and she could feel it as our bodies pressed together. Then she pulled away.
'Eat your eggs,' she ordered.
'They can wait.'
'Now.'
It was my turn to shrug. 'Do you want some? I've done enough for two.'
'Okay.' She took out another plate and helped herself.
We ate in silence for a few moments.
'What was all the excitement over before I started making trouble?' I asked.

She thought for a moment, obviously trying to decide if I could be trusted. 'Vernon Duke has been receiving crank calls, death threats, now, suddenly, everyone is taking it seriously. He's gone under deep wraps and we have all the stops out to try to find who's behind it.'

'Here?'

She nodded. 'His office is on Wilshire and he has a home north of the city, in San Fernando.'

'Any ideas who's behind the threats?'

'It could be anyone, logic isn't part of an assassin's stock in trade these days.'

I suppose not; it wasn't an area where I felt competent to even offer a comment.

'By the way,' she went on, 'Terita Montez didn't report the break-in at her house. Did you make it without leaving any sign?'

I thought about the smashed window. 'No, she must have known.'

'So the chances are she'll tie me in with it.'

'Could be.'

She sighed. 'Ah, well, early retirement should leave me free to earn a better, safer living someplace else.' She ate some more. 'I checked the Meridian; they didn't report anything happening there either, apart from the stolen ambulance.'

'Interesting.'

'And we have an identification of the gunman.'

'You do?' She was enjoying stretching this out, I could see.

'The TriCity cops found the gun and impounded the ambulance. You were right about a print on the cartridge cases, only partials but enough.'

'Who is he?'

'His name is Rafer Johnson. He's from Philadelphia

and if he isn't wanted at the moment it's simply because he's only been out for a couple of months.'

'What's his racket?'

She smiled. 'You're starting to talk like an old movie cop.'

'Where do you think I did my training? What about Johnson?'

'Mostly robbery but several suspicions of murder that couldn't be proved. The word from Philly is that he's a low-order hit man for the Syndicate.'

'Now you're starting to talk like a cop in the movies.'

She laughed. We were friends again. 'You think Johnson and Roccisano are in this together, whatever it is?'

'They must be. I think Roccisano gave me Leo Collis's name because they were already onto him and didn't much care if I got my nose in front. I think he must've called Johnson as soon as I ditched him at LAX and was probably in the car that chased us. When you dig the bullets out of Leo and the hotel wall you'll find at least two different weapons, probably different calibre.' I took Roccisano's gun out. 'This wasn't one of them but maybe you should take it in case it's been used for anything else.' I laid the gun on the table between us.

'Who were they shooting at?'

I told her what I'd worked out last night; that Linda was still top of their list but I was treading on toes.

'Do you know why?'

I shook my head. I reached into my other pocket and took out the cake of soap. I told her about the hidden room at Terita Montez's house and the video camera and the one-way mirror and the extra key. She looked at the impression and at the numbers I'd written down separately.

'I think it's a baggage-locker key.' Standing up, she

went through into the other room. I heard her dialling and speaking at the same time.

Barbara Collis came into the kitchen. She was wearing a towelling wrap that belonged to the lieutenant and almost drowned her. She looked younger and tinier than ever. I remembered how Ella had looked younger each time I'd seen her, right up until the last time, when she was dead.

'Is she your girl?' she asked me.

I glanced at the door through which I could hear the lieutenant speaking on the phone. 'Not exactly,' I said.

'I told her we were together last night. Was that wrong?'

'It's okay,' I said.

'Thank you,' she said softly.

'For what?'

'For saving my life and for not, well, thank you.'

I grinned. 'Don't take any chances and make that kind of offer again,' I warned her. 'Next time I might let nature take its course.'

She giggled, then was abruptly serious.

'You'll make out,' I said, trying to sound more confident than I felt. I had a vision of her future. More nude dancing until her figure went or she ran out of seedy bars to work in, then a little casual hooking on the side, then before she knew it there would be a pimp with eyes for more money and soon she would be turning tricks as fast as the johns could zip their trousers, then the disease and maybe the drugs to make the pain and the sadness go away and then – nothing.

Lieutenant Bercovici came back. Something in my face must have told her I was having gloomy thoughts because she glanced from me to the tiny black girl and back again. I summoned up a smile.

'Are you hungry?' she asked Barbara.

She shook her head.

'Can she stay here?' I asked.

The lieutenant glanced at me sideways and something like a grin flickered on her lips. 'Of course,' she said.

'I don't want to be in the way,' Barbara said.

'Don't worry about it. Come along, I'll show you my daughter's room and you can use some of her clothes. They may be a size too big but there should be something that will do for now.'

They went out of the kitchen and I spent the next few minutes being domestic, washing plates and the pan, then I made coffee. It was ready when the lieutenant came down again.

'The key is for a baggage locker at the bus depot in Santa Monica,' she told me. She handed over a piece of paper. 'That's the address of a man who will make a duplicate for you. I'll call him and tell him you're one of us.'

'I've no car,' I reminded her.

'Use mine today, but you'd better make arrangements from tomorrow. About someplace to stay as well.'

'Can't I stay here?'

She grinned. 'We don't what that young girl corrupted, do we?'

I glowered at her. 'That's a lousy trick to pull.'

'You're the one who asked if she could stay here.'

'You're hard, Lieutenant Bercovici, do you know that?'

'I know it, and now so do you.'

She was enjoying my irritation but I wasn't convinced she would really push it.

'Okay,' I said. 'Car keys, please.'

She went through into the living room with me following and took her keys from a soft brown leather bag.

'Try not to have this one burnt or shot up, will you?'

'I'll do my best,' I assured her. 'By the way, speaking of all that, can you find the rental car and have it taken back or whatever seems best.' I gave her a rough idea of where to find it. I decided that I should really have to find a different rental firm for the next one. And somehow persuade someone to make peace with the first outfit. I didn't want them hounding me back to Liverpool with claims for payment. The Chief Constable and I had little enough in common as it was, there was no point in giving him ammunition.

'I'll try finding out a little more about the Meridian,' she told me. 'In between hunting down potential assassins and covering up last night's depredations by an unknown desperado.'

'You're working today?'

'This afternoon. I'll hitch a ride in a prowl car and don't worry about Barbara, she'll be okay.'

'Try doing something about the other girl, will you?'

'Stop worrying, Mace.'

I kissed her on the tip of the nose again. She looked up at me. 'Be careful,' she said.

'All I'm doing is looking in a baggage locker. Even I can't turn that into World War Three.'

'Hmmm. I'm not so sure about that.'

I kissed her, on the lips this time and her response almost made me forget about the fact that we had a guest right above us. Then she pushed me away and opened the door and waved me out as if I was an offending small creature that had wandered in from the woods.

I went reluctantly, driving with more care and attention than was usual. I didn't want to continue with my less than fortunate record with her car.

The key maker had a room on the front at Santa Monica where he cut keys and repaired watches and engraved lockets and generally did the kind of thing people like that do all over the world, usually on sea fronts.

If he thought matching a key to an impression in a cake of soap was unusual he was too polite to say so, either that or Lieutenant Bercovici carried too much weight for idle curiosity.

The locker at the depot was one of a batch of maybe fifty. At the first try the key didn't turn but the man who'd made it had warned me of that possibility. I went into the washroom and rubbed it smooth on the edge of a broken wall tile. That done I smeared it in liquid soap and went back for another try. This time it worked.

The locker was empty.

I closed the door, went out to the car and sat in it, thinking.

Then I went back into the depot and looked again. I took out my nailfile, thinking that I was becoming as dependent on that as an alky on his bottle. I ran the file around the edge of the shelf which was of thin sheet steel folded over and riveted through the casing. Halfway along the back I felt something. With a little bit of teasing I lifted it out. Black, half an inch or less wide, three inches long, almost no thickness at all. Shiny on one side, less shiny on the other. Like a piece of tape. It *was* a piece of tape. Video tape.

Back in the car I held the tape up to the light to check that it wasn't really film. Nothing, just black tape. I chewed the problem over, then had an idea that might turn out to be bright.

Twenty minutes later I was at Helen Jerome's house talking to her over her intercom. She let me in and was delighted to see me and even more so when I told her I needed help.

Her film editing equipment was still out and she sat down at the table studying my piece of tape. 'It's not like film, you know,' she said.

'I know, but it's worth a try. Do you have a video machine?'

She had, in the living room under a table that groaned under the weight of a giant colour TV and a small mountain of books almost all of which appeared to be on cinema.

'Now you know my secret vices,' she said.

'All of them?'

She laughed. 'Ah, Mr Mace, what it would be like to be young again.'

We brought a cassette out, one that she said wouldn't matter if it was damaged. I fiddled with the plastic case and eased out a loop of tape a few feet long. Checking the size it looked as if we had a match.

'Anything I can do?' I asked.

'No, leave it to me,' she said.

I did as I was instructed, and went into the kitchen to try making a cup of real copper's tea. I almost succeeded although the absence of a suitably encrusted teapot conspired to make the results less than perfect. By the time I was finished so was she.

'I think we should let it dry longer than usual,' she suggested. 'I'm not sure if the cement works the same on tape as on film.'

We sat there, drinking tea, with Helen Jerome politely not saying what her expression clearly indicated: that she didn't much care for copper's tea.

Then I put the cassette back the way it was and we went into the living room, turned on the TV and the recorder and slotted in the cassette.

The strip was so short it passed too quickly to be seen clearly but I took it back on the slow re-wind, then used the still-frame button to hold the picture on one of the frames Helen had spliced in. It was upside down so I doubled over to look.

Ordinarily it wasn't a picture that would have raised any eyebrows. A close up of two people, only heads visible. Both smiling brightly. One young, a boy of about thirteen, blond and blue-eyed. He looked happy and healthy. The other was a man, also happy and looking fit. Even white teeth gleamed in a tanned face beneath prematurely white hair.

I recognised him from the TV newscast I'd seen last Monday night and from the vote-catching smile he'd given me when I was leaving The Tail of the Cock that same night.

It was Vernon Duke, candidate for election as Governor of California.

Chapter Ten

I called the lieutenant's home but it was Barbara who answered the phone.

'She's gone, Mr Mace.'

'Okay, thanks, Barbara, I'll call her at the station. Are you okay?'

'Sure. This is nice.'

I guessed she meant spending time in a comfortable home without having to pay dearly for it. It crossed my mind that with one thing and another I had never got around to asking her the question outright, the one that started all last night's gunplay. I asked her now.

'No, I'm sorry, Linda and me, we weren't close. Not like her and Ella. She wouldn't say to me where she would go.'

'No special friends?'

I listened to a hum of static while she thought. 'She had a friend, a boyfriend. Nothing serious but he liked her a lot, I could tell.'

'What's his name?'

More static. 'Gary, I think. I don't know his last name.'

'Where does he live?'

'I don't know.'

This wasn't getting very far.

'He's a musician,' Barbara added helpfully.

'Where does he play?'

'Around.'

I gritted my teeth to keep from yelling. 'Does he play in a band?'

'Yes.'

'What kind of band?'

'A rock band. Gary plays guitar.'

'Do you know the band's name?'

'The Hurricanes or the Whirlwinds or something like that.'

'Can you describe him?'

'He's tall, has long blond hair, kind of nice looking.'

'Anything else?'

'No, sorry, Mr Mace.'

'That's okay, Barbara. Take care, I'll see you later. Oh, listen, don't talk to anyone or let anyone in the house, will you.'

'No, don't worry about me, the lieutenant has told the police to come by during the day to see that I'm okay.'

We hung up and I thought about what she'd told me.

Linda had a friend who played in a rock band and was named Gary. There couldn't be more than a thousand rock bands in Greater Los Angeles and there wouldn't be more than two members of each band named Gary and since all of them would be blond and kind of nice looking and play guitar it would be easy to find him.

Like hell it would.

Then I stopped being surly. At least I had something, whereas before I'd had nothing at all. The trouble was, I couldn't see how to capitalise on the information.

I called Lieutenant Bercovici's office but she was at a briefing and I was asked to call back in about an hour. I said I would and after picking up the cassette and saying thanks and goodbye to Helen Jerome I drove down towards the gates. Just before I reached them another car went past on the street. Terita Montez was driving.

I followed her on impulse because while I knew less and less about what was going on, the clip of video tape suggested that she knew more than I'd supposed.

The Sunday afternoon traffic was thin and the sun was hot and the sky an unbroken cerulean expanse that looked as if it went on forever. It was the kind of day to be taking a drive in the country with a beautiful woman and a picnic hamper filled with caviar and champagne. Instead I was trailing a maker of pornographic movies who was somehow tied in with a growing list of killings. It didn't seem right.

We dropped down onto Mulholland, went west and eventually she turned into Beverly Glen Boulevard which led up into Brown Canyon. There were turnings off to both sides, each with neatly-painted little boards indicating that every turning led to half a dozen additional streets. I closed up, if I missed any turn she might make I'd have a hard job picking her up again.

The road narrowed at one point and I had to hang back to let an ivory Rolls-Royce come through. The driver was a young woman with white-blonde hair tied back with a piece of green shot-silk. She was wearing a fluffy angora sweater that exactly matched the colour of her hair and the colour of the car. I wondered whether she'd dyed her hair to match the Roller or if the paint job had been customised to suit her hair. She floated past me as if I was invisible and I suppose to her I was.

When the road was clear again Terita Montez was invisible too.

I pushed the lieutenant's car ahead until I was sure that Terita was no longer on the main road. I turned and went back to the point where I'd stopped for the white car, counting turnings. Four on each side, each leading to a total of twenty-three other streets. I made a desultory tour but it was hopeless.

I drifted back up the canyon, irritated with myself for losing what should have been a simple tail.

At the top of the road I stopped and rummaged in the lieutenant's glove box and came up with a street map that was even more well-thumbed that the one I'd left behind in one or another of my rental cars.

It was now mid-afternoon and I had a vague recollection that sometimes musicians used Carmelo's for rehearsals at this time on Sundays. I was hungry, needed a drink and also wanted someplace from which to call Lieutenant Bercovici so I drove over there.

The street door was closed and locked but I could hear music and went around the back and in the service entrance. Before anyone had a chance to throw me out I saw Bill Berry and went over to talk, hoping he would protect me from ejection.

The band rehearsing was the Bob Florence Big Band preparing for a date that night at the Anson Ford Theatre. Bill wasn't involved, just killing a little time before driving to the airport to pick up his wife Betty who was coming in from Cincinnati later in the day.

'I have a few dates out there next week,' he told me. 'Betty is smoothing the way.'

'I could use someone to smooth the way for me,' I said.

'Trouble?'

There was nothing much I could tell him without involving him in a very messy and dangerous business so I changed the subject, asking if he knew anything about the local rock scene. He didn't but was interested enough to ask why. I told him I was looking for a rock musician named Gary.

'Tell me what you know and I'll ask my son,' he said.

'Is he into that kind of music?'

'Not especially, but he's closer to the age group and, who knows, he might come up with something.'

I told him what little I knew and he wrote it down. I added Lieutenant Bercovici's home and office numbers and then, for what it was worth, asked him about the bartender from The Blue Whale. No bells rang but a couple of the people who ran the club were there and Bill hauled them over. I described the bartender as best I could and told them his name was Corelli.

'I remember the guy,' one of them said. 'I noticed the eyebrows, looked as though he'd done ten rounds with Sugar Ray *and* Ali. He's been in here a couple of times but I don't think it was for the music. Most times he met someone and then left. I can't recall if he met anyone last Monday.'

'Can you describe any of the people he met?'

He thought about that for a while, then shook his head.

'I saw him someplace else once,' the other guy chimed in. 'I was working a private party up in Bel Air. He was there.'

'Was he working with you?'

'Him? Hell, no, he was a guest.'

I thought about that. 'Where in Bel Air?'

'Somewhere in Stone Canyon. People named McQuaid.'

They went off to rearrange the tables or whatever it was they were doing. Bill was looking at me curiously. 'Did that help?' he asked.

'I have a feeling it did,' I said. 'But I'm not sure how.'

The band was whipping into a snappy performance of 'Party Hearty' boosted by some fluid drumming from Nick Ceroli. I hated to leave but I had that churning feeling in my stomach that sometimes comes on a case. There's no reason for it, no logical cold clear reason but it's there all the same and the only thing to do about it is to work and work and work until something pops.

I said goodbye to Bill and he assured me that he'd get Bill Jr. onto my rock musician as soon as possible. As I went out back to my car Bob Cooper and Pete Christlieb were really blowing and I had their music in my ears all the way back to Pandora Avenue.

Barbara let me in and I asked her about the private parties the girls sometimes played. She remembered working at several in Bel Air but Corelli hadn't been at any of them although he seemed to be at back of most of the dates the girls worked. The name McQuaid meant nothing to her but I wasn't too worried about that because it meant something to me.

I called the lieutenant's office. The briefing was over but she'd gone straight out. I asked where.

'I can't divulge that information,' the voice on the line told me.

'It's important,' I said. 'Look, can you reach her and tell her that Mace wants to talk with her right away.'

'Oh, you're Mr Mace,' the voice said brightly. 'The lieutenant left a message for you.' There was a pause, then the voice came back on. 'She said she was driving out to Arrowhead Springs and that you would understand.'

I didn't know what the hell she was talking about. 'Is that all?'

'Yes, sir.'

'Thanks,' I said and hung up.

I went out to the car and pulled out a map. I found Arrowhead Springs just north of San Bernardino. I hadn't known but that was the location of the Meridian Home for the Mentally Handicapped.

It was over a hundred miles but with freeways most of the way I made good time by stretching the speed limit at every opportunity. Even so it was early evening and the sun was hanging low in the sky behind me when I drove back up the road I'd raced down in the ambulance.

I parked in the trees a short distance from the gates. I could see a uniformed guard patrolling inside. Security had been tightened.

I left the car, wishing I had kept Roccisano's gun, and tried my hand at woodcraft. I made it to the shadow of the wall without setting off any alarm bells. I worked my way along the wall until I was well clear of the gate, trying to recall as best I could the little amount I knew about the layout of the hospital. I was some distance beyond where I'd been held when I came upon a steel manhole set into a pad of concrete about ten feet from the wall. Hooking my fingers into the tool-holes I managed to lift the cover high enough to edge a twig under with my foot. Then I was able to lift the edge and peer down.

There was a smooth-sided concrete tunnel about two feet in diameter. A small trickle of clean water ran along the bottom, through the opening and on into another similar tunnel that pointed down the hill. I guessed it was some kind of drainage channel.

I knew I was taking a chance but I eased myself into the hole, closed the lid carefully above me and crawled along the tunnel as fast as I could, trying not to think too much about what kind of effluent could come streaming along towards me at any moment.

I had gone maybe fifty yards when I came to a junction with another tunnel and at that point a chamber similar to the one I'd entered by. I reached up, pushed at the cover and peered out. I could see buildings all around me and I could also hear voices.

Then I heard another sound, water rushing. I pushed the cover higher, slid out and ran for the nearest building. I made it and straightened up, feeling my water-sodden trousers cling to my legs. It was a small price to pay;

judging from the rush of water I'd heard coming along the tunnel something much worse might have happened if I hadn't got out when I did.

I took a cautious look around. I was in a corner between a single-storey white-painted building and a much taller structure built from red bricks. There was a door a few feet away and I opened it, peeped in, then went swiftly inside. The brick building was a laundry and kitchen complex. I tried another door. Some people were working at machines. They had their backs to me. The machines were heavy-duty steam presses. Just behind them, some ten feet from me, were piles of neatly laundered white coats. I took two quick, long paces, reached out a hand, grabbed the top garment off the pile and went back and out.

I slipped the coat on. It didn't make me look like a doctor but at least it covered all but the last few inches of my wet clothes.

I marched along a corridor, trying to look as if I had shares in the company that owned the place, hoping to quickly figure out where the lieutenant might be, always assuming that she was in the building at all.

I came out of the laundry-kitchen complex and into a high-ceilinged lobby. I guessed this was the main entrance. A door opened and a young woman in white came out and walked past me with a friendly nod of the head. I returned the gesture and went straight in through the same door. It was an office, empty of people but I could hear voices coming from behind a glass-panelled door.

I listened, didn't recognise any of the voices, and went out again. I realised that I was floundering. I didn't know if the lieutenant was here, if she was I didn't know if she was calling officially or not, I didn't know why she was here. I didn't know anything, except that I had broken into a nuthouse from which I would soon have to break out – for the second time.

I went across the entrance lobby and poked my head around another door. The room beyond was filled with filing cabinets, three rows of them. One up against each of the two longest walls, the third down the middle of the room.

I was about to close the door again when a foot scraped on the floor at the far end of the room. Someone was there, hiding from me. I couldn't take the risk of leaving. Whoever it was could give the alarm and I would be sunk.

I closed the door, throwing the room into near-darkness. Swiftly I went down between two rows of cabinets ready for anything.

I wasn't ready for the sight that greeted me. Lieutenant Bercovici was crouched down against the wall, her revolver pointing up into my face.

'For God's sake, Mace,' she said. 'I might have blown your head off.'

I took a deep breath and reached out to turn the gun away. 'Fancy meeting you here,' I said, trying to be casual but aware of a pulse hammering in my head. A revolver pointing at a man from a couple of feet away has that effect, even when it's held by a friend.

'How did you get in?' she asked.

'With difficulty. How about you?'

'I came in with the afternoon visitors, then hid until it quietened down for the evening.'

'Why?'

'I told you I would be asking more questions about this place. Well, I found two things. One is that the owners of the Meridian have friends in high places. I was told very firmly to keep my nose out of San Bernardino's affairs and that even the local pd wouldn't ask questions here.'

'What questions did you want to ask?'

'That was the other thing I found out. Your little friend Clara King spent time here years ago.'

I remembered Helen Jerome telling me that the midget had killed her baby. 'Interesting,' I said. 'But not enough to put your job on the line.'

'She's here again,' the lieutenant said.

'Clara?'

She nodded. I couldn't make out her expression in the darkness.

'What are you doing in this room?' I asked.

'Main files of all the patients. I thought I'd take a look at Clara's case notes.'

'Have you found them yet?'

'Just before you came in.' She rustled something at me.

'Maybe we should look at them here, then we can leave them behind when we go. That way no one gets suspicious.'

'Turn the light on.'

I did so. The lieutenant spread a folder on top of a cabinet and sifted through the pages.

Breaking down the contents into plain language it appeared that Clara had never really been cured of the problem that had driven her to dismember her newborn child and throw the bits onto a fire. Given the opportunity she would be liable to try something similarly unpleasant at any time; the file didn't seem to think she'd actually done so but over the years there had been several relapses and brief incarcerations at the Meridian.

'She was born in Philadelphia,' I remarked, reading the original committal notes.

'So?'

'So just about everyone I've met on this case seems to come from there. Roccisano, Rafer Johnson, now Clara.'

'It's a big town.' She didn't appear to think it significant. Turning over more pages Lieutenant

Bercovici read off the latest admission details. Clara had been admitted here during the previous night and was presently in Room 704.

I had noticed something else. Clara King had been brought in by a man named Tom McQuaid. Life, it seemed, was chockful of strange little coincidences.

Then, before I had a chance to say so to the lieutenant, footsteps echoed outside and the door opened. Two men stood there, white-coated and built to withstand the efforts of the biggest and toughest cases the Meridian was likely to handle.

'Who the hell are you?' one asked. He had a face like wet sponge. Yellow, wet and pockmarked.

I stood up straight so he could see my white coat. 'Doctor Welby,' I told him.

He stared at me, then looked at his companion who had the unblinking stare of a long-dead lizard. 'We ain't got no Doctor Welby,' the lizard said.

I walked briskly towards him. 'I'm new around here,' I said. 'Joined the strength only this morning.' Behind me I could hear the lieutenant was keeping close.

'I think I heard the name,' the sponge was saying.

I pushed between them and kept on moving with Lieutenant Bercovici now striding along by my side. I picked up some signs and followed those marked with a '7' hoping to reach Room 704 before the roof fell in.

'Welby,' the lieutenant said disgustedly. 'Why not Kildare?'

'He didn't handle nutcases,' I told her.

'What an imagination.'

We were in the single-storey building that adjoined the kitchen and laundry block.

'This had better be fast,' I said. 'Mutt and Jeff won't keep our presence to themselves for long.'

We were outside 704 now. A small glass panel was let

into the door. I looked inside. Mainly white, the room was small and well-equipped with bed and chairs and TV and even a big bunch of flowers. Clara King lay in the bed, her eyes were closed. I tried the handle and the door opened.

Inside I crossed to the bed and leaned over the little woman. She was sleeping. The lieutenant joined me. She touched Clara. There was a movement but the eyes didn't open. The lieutenant bent her head and sniffed at Clara's lips which made her braver than me.

'Drugged,' she said.

'Damn,' I said.

'Drugged,' Clara King said in a cracked whisper.

I looked at Lieutenant Bercovici and she looked at me.

'Try asking her a question,' I suggested.

'What's your name?' she said to the woman in the bed.

'Clara King.'

'Why are you here?'

'Shouldn't be here. Said I killed her. My baby. Didn't kill her.' Something horribly like a laugh trickled from her dry throat. 'I cut her up and burned her but he killed her. Not me.'

I looked at the lieutenant. She was looking as puzzled as I felt.

'Who killed your baby?' I asked.

Far off I heard a bell ring.

'Killed her,' Clara said.

'Who did?'

Tears formed at the corners of her closed eyes and began to roll down her parchment-like skin.

'Was it McQuaid?' I asked, ignoring Lieutenant Bercovici's enquiring glance.

The bell was still ringing.

'How about Roccisano?' I tried.

Nothing, just more tears.

'Corelli?' I was getting desperate.

'Bastard,' Clara said. 'Him and Terry, both bastards.'

Then Lieutenant Bercovici wasn't beside me. She was at the door listening, I could hear it too. Footsteps, running, getting closer.

'Who killed the baby?' I yelled at Clara.

Suddenly her eyes blinked open and she screamed loud and long.

'Mace!'

I turned, fast. The lieutenant was going out the door, gun in hand. There was a confusion of yells and bells ringing and right in my ear Clara King was still screeching. I went out into the corridor at a run.

Mutt and Jeff were there, backing up slowly with hands raised and watchful but unafraid eyes on the lieutenant's gun.

I checked the other way along the corridor. It seemed clear. I moved that way with the lieutenant following, her back to me, the revolver still aimed steadily at the heavy mob.

I tried every door we came to, at last finding one that had what I was looking for. I gestured to the two men. 'In there,' I ordered.

They edged into the room and I slammed the door closed.

'That should keep them for a while, there's no handle on the inside.'

I set off back the way we'd come.

'Where are you going?'

'Unless you plan on shooting your way out we'll leave by the way I came in.'

She didn't argue and soon we were outside the laundry. I pointed out the manhole cover and left her watching the building for signs of anyone coming after us. The bell had stopped ringing now but there was a lot of shouting going on somewhere in the main offices.

I lifted the manhole and called.

She came over and looked down. 'I'm not going down there.'

'For Christ's sake, this is no time to start an argument.'

'It'll ruin this suit.'

She was wearing a mid-blue two piece suit cut slightly mannish, a high-necked white blouse and a darker blue string tie.

'Just when I thought you were different to all the other women I've ever met you have to say something like that,' I said.

She glared at me, pushed past and lowered herself down. I followed, directing her by touch into the tunnel I'd come along.

She was ahead of me and I couldn't see what I was looking for but I gauged the distance approximately and called out to her when we were close to where I thought the outer manhole should be. Crunched up close together I pushed at the cover and lifted it. Moments later I was outside and helping her up.

It was the fresh, clean air among the trees that made me more aware of the smell in the tunnel. The lieutenant must have noticed it too.

'What the hell do they use that for?' she demanded.

'Try not to think about it,' I suggested. I headed towards where I'd left the car, moving fast, anxious to get out of the area. I was too anxious, and too careless.

I was almost at the car when I heard a sound ahead of me. I stopped dead in my tracks but I was too late. Standing at the car, leaning nonchalantly against the front wing was a very tall man. As a glimmer of moonlight brightened up the scene I recognised the black hit man from Philadelphia, his jaw still strapped up.

'Well, now, fancy meeting you,' Rafer Johnson said.

I could also see he was pointing a gun at me. It looked very steady.

'You got more lives than five cats,' he told me. 'Only your luck just ran out.' He touched his broken jaw reflectively.

I tried to hear what the lieutenant was doing. I couldn't even hear her breathing.

Johnson straightened up and moved closer, I heard the dry click as he thumbed back the hammer.

I tensed, ready to dive sideways when something struck the side of the car with a light metallic click.

Johnson spun around and fired all in one fluid movement.

I was also moving, going to my left into the trees.

'Freeze, Johnson,' Lieutenant Bercovici called from somewhere to my right.

He didn't. He loosed off a shot in the direction of her voice, then spun around and saw me. His gun was up and he was ready to go again when the lieutenant's gun boomed out of the shadows and it was Rafer Johnson's luck that ran out.

The bullet hit him square in the chest throwing him backwards as if he'd been hit by an Amtrak express. He hit the ground in an explosion of leaves and lay still.

I moved forward, picking up his fallen gun and checked his neck for a pulse but it was a needless gesture and I knew it.

The lieutenant came over, her gun hand hanging straight down by her side. Her face looked unnaturally pale in the moonlight but I didn't think that was the cause. I couldn't know if she'd done it before but even if she had, killing a man, even a man like Rafer Johnson, wasn't something to rejoice over.

I could hear shouts now, from inside the wall. I took her arm and pulled her towards the car. Moments later we were on the road, heading fast towards San Bernardino and the long drive back to her home in Century City.

Maybe the couple of hours or so that would take would help settle her down. On the other hand, maybe she would never fully accept killing. I didn't want her to suffer, but in a way I hoped she would find it hard to accept. To do otherwise would make her harder than I wanted her to be.

Chapter Eleven

We spoke only once on the drive back. Somewhere around Pasadena she asked me why I'd asked Clara about a man named McQuaid.

I told her that was the name of the man who'd brought her to the hospital, that a man with the same name lived in Bel Air which was near where I'd trailed Terita Montez and who gave parties to which Corelli the bartender sent girls from The Blue Whale. I also told her that it was a man named McQuaid from the Governor's staff who had very generously offered to pay compensation for damage both of us knew he hadn't done.

She didn't say anything about the coincidence of a not very common name and although there were many things I wanted to talk to her about I deemed it wiser to hold off until she was out of the state of mild shock I had decided she was in. Now I really was trying to act like Marcus Welby, M.D.

At the house we went in silently but even so Barbara heard us. She came downstairs, looked at our faces in silence and went back to bed again. I looked in a mirror and I saw tight lips, set cheeks, tired eyes. Lieutenant Bercovici looked the same way.

The lieutenant went upstairs to shower and change out

of her messed-up clothing and after she'd come down again, now dressed in the brown velvet robe I'd seen before, I used the shower too. Not wanting to climb back into my reeking and wet clothes I fished around until I found a towelling robe that wasn't too feminine even if it was several sizes too small.

When I came down again the lieutenant had poured out two giant-sized whiskeys, and I had the impression hers was a refill.

'Was he your first?' I asked.

She nodded.

'I know how you feel,' I told her. 'And it won't get any easier.'

'I thought you English policemen didn't carry guns.'

'Most of the time we don't but we're forced into it sometimes. Sad to say, it's getting more usual.'

Neither of us spoke for a few moments.

It was an aspect of policing I didn't like but which had become unavoidable. Liverpool was no worse than many other British cities, in fact it was better than many. But it was the gateway into the country for visitors from Ireland, and those in a hurry to get back there. Recently, they hadn't all been simple wayfarers.

As I said to her, guns were becoming more usual. Not yet commonplace but heading that way. If my experiences of the past few days were an indication of where it was all leading I hoped we would somehow find another course. I didn't fancy living this way for the rest of my life. More to the point, if things really did continue on in this way my working life might find itself abruptly and unpleasantly terminated.

It crossed my mind that there might be more to life than police work. Looking at the lieutenant, beautiful and pale, her shadowed eyes filled with sadness, I knew there could be an alternative.

I had made an irrevocable promise to myself when the divorce was finalised: no more permanant relationships, they screwed up the job. But, if the job ended . . .

'Why are you sitting over there?' she asked after some time.

She was on the cream leather couch and I was on one of the armchairs. I moved across and sat next to her. She leaned her head against me and I wrapped an arm over her shoulders.

'I'll have some explaining to do,' she said. 'Not only was I outside my jurisdiction but I'd been specifically told not to go there. Add to that the fact that I killed a man and failed to report it right away and I guess my badge will be on the commissioner's desk before the week is out.'

'Don't rush it,' I said. 'There's more here than we think there is.'

I told her about the scrap of video tape and the picture of Vernon Duke.

'What does it mean?' she asked.

'I don't know but how sure are you that this story about Duke's life being threatened is true?'

'What are you driving at?'

'Suppose that it isn't an assassination but a kidnap. If someone has kidnapped Duke, the story that he's in hiding could be a cover to account for the fact that he's not around and for all the extra police activity.'

She shook her head. 'Surely word would have leaked.'

'Not necessarily and don't say someone would've told you. This would be a job for top brass only with a strict need-to-know only clamp-down on lower ranks.'

'And you think that Terita Montez is mixed up in it?'

'She has a video picture of him.'

'That's a pretty big leap of conjecture.'

I sighed and swallowed more of my drink. She was right, I was leaping to unlikely conclusions.

'Anyway, who would the boy be?'

'His son?' I suggested.

'He has no children. His wife's quite a few years older than he is. Opponents say he married her for her money. Her father was a brewing baron in . . .' Her voice trailed off.

'Don't tell me; Philadelphia.'

'Yes.'

I shook my head wearily. I felt like a man with half a dozen pieces left over from a jigsaw puzzle and none of them would fit unless banged in with the heel of a shoe.

I started to get up off the couch.

'Where are you going?'

'For the phone book, I want to look up McQuaid's address.'

'We're not going out there tonight.' It wasn't a question, it was a command.

'No,' I agreed, settling back. 'We're not going out there tonight.'

She slipped a hand inside the robe, then, surprisingly, she giggled.

'What is it?'

'You look damn silly in that thing,' she said. 'Take it off.'

'We have a guest upstairs, remember.'

'Damn you, Mace, I want to be fucked. Now.'

There are times to argue and times not to argue. This was clearly among the latter.

I took off the robe which was already proving useless to hide my enthusiasm. Just as quickly she was out of hers and we rolled onto the floor together in an embrace that a Cumberland wrestler couldn't have bettered for power.

I tried to kiss and caress her but she was pulling at me, her arms wrapped around me, her legs spread wide apart.

'Now,' she said. 'Don't wait. Now, dammit.'

I entered her and she was so excited that it was as though her insides were running wet with warm syrup.

It was fast and it was exciting and it was over much too soon but it was what she wanted.

As we both subsided her grip weakened but didn't loosen altogether. Her body was shaking and I knew that she was crying.

After a long time she stopped and pushed gently at me. I eased up and out of her and we sat side by side on the floor, our back resting against the couch.

'I feel lousy,' she said. 'I killed a man and all it's done is make me horny.'

'Don't think about it,' I said. 'A reaction is a reaction, it doesn't have to make sense or be something you'd tell your mother about.'

'Let's got to bed,' she said.

Once again I didn't see any cause to argue with her. Standing up I helped her to her feet. She was shaking slightly. I held her close and kissed the tip of her nose. 'I can't go on calling you lieutenant,' I said.

She managed a slightly tremulous smile. 'From now on you can call me darling, except when I'm on duty.'

'I thought cops were always on duty.'

'Can you see my badge?'

I held her away from me and let my eyes drift over her beautiful body. 'Not unless you keep it in a very peculiar place,' I said. 'And I have to admit, if it's there, I didn't feel it.'

'Come on,' she said. 'Bed.'

'Yes, lieutenant, darling,' I said.

Next morning Barbara had beaten us all to it and was frying in the kitchen. From the smell it could've been anything but whatever it was I was starving hungry. So was the lieutenant but we found a very good reason not to hurry down.

Later, having eaten under the amused and wordly eyes of the tiny black girl we ate, drank half a gallon of coffee between the three of us and were ready to face the world.

The lieutenant wore black today. It seemed appropriate.

I asked her to drive by the clothing store where the assistant couldn't conceal his curiosity any longer about the way I treated my clothes.

'I wreck cars for a living,' I told him. It was very nearly true.

We had an address for a Tom McQuaid courtesy of the phone book. It was in Vestone Way off Stone Canyon Road. A Beverly Hills prowl car was nosing around the area as we drove up and Lieutenant Bercovici took this particular bull by the horns and told the guy that we were checking out a reported burglary.

He grumbled that no one had told him but didn't push it when the lieutenant told him we wanted to take a look around the McQuaid house's grounds. But he came with us, after remarking that McQuaid himself was away on election business. The phone number in the book had already confirmed that this was the same McQuaid who'd made an offer to me via the rental company. We still didn't know if it was the same McQuaid who'd checked Clara King into the hospital, nor that it was where the girls came for parties. Barbara Collis hadn't been able to help us there; visits always were made at night and up here, she'd said, one house looked pretty much like another.

From what I could see that wasn't right, the houses were all very different architecturally speaking but I think I know what she meant. They were all big and lost among trees.

We wandered around the grounds and learned absolutely nothing. Then, while the lieutenant conversed animatedly with the uniformed cop in a way that made him think he'd finally made the bigtime, I drifted closer to the house.

A large picture window only slightly smaller than the three-car garage door let me look into a room that must have cost more to carpet than most people pay for their entire homes. Vernon Duke must pay his staff well, I thought.

I was turning away when something just inside the window caught my eye. It was oddly out of place. An army-style field telephone. I scowled at it, thinking. Then I put my face right up to the glass and followed the wire with my eyes. It came out through a tiny hole drilled very close to the ground.

I followed the wire but after about a yard it went down into the lawn. I strolled away from the house across a smooth acre of immaculately manicured grass, past a deodar tree that cast the only patch of shade from the strong sun and eventually reached a wire fence that appeared to mark the end of McQuaid's territory.

I walked along the fence, backwards and forwards a couple of times before I spotted the wire coming up out of the ground a few feet over the boundary. It climbed a tree, then disappeared through the leaves in a long curving loop towards another tree trunk.

I couldn't see another house but there had to be one there.

I went back and rescued Lieutenant Bercovici from the cop who was almost purple with enthusiasm.

In her car I studied the map while telling her what I'd found.

'Why a field telephone?'

'I don't know, except they must be tricky things to bug.'

She looked at the map with me. 'Well?'

'The other house must be about there,' I pointed. 'Bel-

Air Road and that is right slap in the area where I lost Terita Montez yesterday.'

She started the engine and we drove round to the other road. It took quite a while because we had to go all the way back up Stone Canyon to Sunset before we could swing round and into Brown Canyon.

If anything the houses in Bel-Air Road were bigger than those we'd seen earlier. They were so well apart from each other than it didn't prove difficult to pinpoint the one with the landline link to the McQuaid house.

It was immense, approximately Gothic, with turrets and corner bay windows all decked out in leaded glass.

'Now what?' the lieutenant asked.

'I guess we break in.'

She opened her mouth to protest but I leaned across and kissed her. She didn't resist.

'If we don't crack this soon you'll be out on your ear anyway. Let's go for broke.'

She sighed. 'My mother warned me about men like you.'

Out of the car we walked hurriedly along the high wall, hoping no car would come along. In this neighbourhood walking was an arrestable offence.

I found a place that looked promising and sent the lieutenant back for the car. When she had manoeuvred it close in by the wall I scrambled up onto the wing and helped her up beside me. Then onto the roof from where I could see over the wall.

'For heaven's sake, Mace. Not dressed like this.'

'Stop worrying about how you look. You'd be great in a sack.' I grinned at her. 'As I already know.'

'Stop talking and get over the goddamn wall.'

Nothing moved in the grounds of the big house and I went over and dropped to the ground. Moments later she lowered herself down, showing me all of her long and lovely legs.

She knew what I was grinning at and struck off right away towards the house, trying hard to be angry.

I hurried after her, concerned that we should really be taking things slightly more circumspectly. But no one shot at us, or set the dogs on us, no whistles blew or sirens wailed.

The house had a pool that would have served for Olympic trials and was surrounded by heavy wrought-iron furniture painted white. No plastic for this poolside. A matching high diving board loomed beside a glassfronted bar, a shower room and other of life's necessities. Then we reached the house.

Music was playing inside; lots of electronics. I tried the sliding doors that overlooked the pool but they refused to slide. I tried a few more doors and windows, gradually getting closer to the room from where the music was coming.

Looking cautiously in through the window I could see someone lying on a deep-pile rug. I had the uneasy thought that I had found yet another corpse when the figure moved and sat up, looking directly at me. It was Terita Montez. Her mouth opened and I prepared to take to the hills but if any sound came out I certainly couldn't hear it.

Slowly, she climbed to her feet and came over to the window. She was wearing a black lace blouse and black trousers with silver stitching down the seam.

She opened the window and looked at me without speaking. She looked awful. She also stank of bourbon.

'I might've known you'd figure it out,' she said eventually.

Turning away she wandered unsteadily back towards the rug and slumped down on it.

I waved to the lieutenant, then scrambled through the window.

'Who else is in the house?' I asked Terita.

'No one. He's out of town.'

I was about to ask who he was when the lieutenant arrived and I broke off to help her through the open window.

'Nice house,' I remarked, hoping to let her tell me who owned the place without having to ask.

'Corelli always did take care of himself,' she said.

I stared at her, then at Lieutenant Bercovici. Corelli? The bartender?

'Back in Philly, he didn't live like this,' I heard myself saying.

Terita shook her head drunkenly. 'Jesus, no, there he scuffled like the rest of us.'

I looked at the lieutenant and raised an eyebrow but she wasn't any brighter than I was.

'Tell me about it,' I said.

Terita looked at me. 'I need another drink,' she said.

Lieutenant Bercovici went over to a tray that stood on a solid Peruvian mahogany table and emptied the dregs from a pint of bourbon into a clean glass. I picked another glass up off the floor. It was smeared with lipstick and hairs from the rug. I don't suppose it presented a health hazard, the spirit would have killed any germs.

'That's where you all knew one another was it, Philadelphia?'

Terita nodded, the movement jerky and uncoordinated.

'You, Clara, Corelli, Roccisano, Johnson.'

Her eyes were none too bright but they grew cloudier as I reeled off my list.

'Didn't know Rocco then, not 'til I hired him to run the films.' She took the glass from the lieutenant, drank most of the contents. 'It was his idea, blackmailing people.'

'That's when you started filming at the house?'

She nodded again, finished off the booze and waved the glass at me. I ignored it.

'You made the videos and Roccisano handled the blackmail. Neat. You get a percentage?'

She didn't respond either way.

I looked up at Lieutenant Bercovici. 'I'm not sure what we're getting here,' I said, 'but it's beginning to make a kind of sense.' I turned back to Terita Montez. 'What happened last Monday night?'

Her head swayed from side to side. 'I don't know, I wasn't there, they said they had something special. I fixed the girls . . . it wasn't me. I didn't want those girls hurt. I don't even know why they did it.' Her voice was rising, getting more strident, contesting with the radio that was still sending out synthesised music.

I got up from the floor beside her and went over to the radio to turn it off but mostly to think.

'Where did you get the strip of video tape?' I asked when I went back to where Terita was now slumping lower on the rug.

'Another drink,' she said.

'Later, when you've told me this.'

'Found it.' Her eyes focussed suddenly. 'How do you know about it?'

'Never mind that. Where did you find it?'

'Rocco had it. When he was drying out.' She began to laugh, a high-pitched hysterical cackle. 'Went into the pool with you.'

'You found it in Roccisano's pockets after the fight?'

She nodded again. 'The bastard was working for Corelli all along. I never knew.'

'Who is Corelli?'

'Bastard.'

'Apart from that.'

'Him and Clara. All his fault, the way she is.'

The lieutenant knelt beside us on the rug. 'Who did Corelli kill?' she asked.

I remembered Clara's whisper in her hospital bed, that she hadn't killed her own baby.

'Corelli was the father of Clara's baby. He left her flat.'

'So who killed the baby?'

A hesitation. 'Nobody killed the baby, she just thinks she did and cut it up and burned the bits.' Her eyes flickered uneasily.

I went in search of another bottle. This time I gave us all a shot. As I came back with the three glasses Terita was trying to stand up, her legs rubbery in their black and silver casing. I'd seen them dressed that way before.

'Why were you at Maria Carreras's apartment the day she was killed?' I asked.

Lieutenant Bercovici looked at me with an enquiring lift to her eyebrow. I grinned and waved a glass under Terita's nose.

'Corelli took Clara there.' Her voice had hardened, she sounded almost sober. 'Clara came back to the house, hysterical. She had blood on her hands, on her clothes. Told me she'd killed a girl. I got the address out of her and went there.' Her face had gone even paler than usual, her stringy neck heaved and for a moment I thought she was about to throw up on the rug. Then she calmed down a little.

'Then I showed up and you slugged me and hopped out the window before the cops arrived.'

She nodded.

'How about Officers Mullany and Carling?' the lieutenant asked.

Terita took the glass from me, two-handed, and drank noisily. 'Lousy cops,' she muttered. 'Always a cop on the take.'

'Do they work for you or Corelli?'

'Me.' The laugh echoed again. 'Corelli buys his own protection.' More laughter, getting hysterical. For some reason this was the biggest joke of all.

'Where's Corelli now?' I asked.

'Airport, Rocco's gone to get him.'

'Which airport?' the lieutenant asked.

Terita was slumping again. I threw the contents of my glass in her face. 'Which airport?' I yelled.

'Van Nuys,' she said and passed out.

I looked up at the lieutenant who was rising to her feet, her glass of bourbon untouched in her hand. I took it from her and swallowed some of the contents. It tasted bitter in my mouth.

'I don't know what we've got,' I said, 'but we've certainly got a lot of it.'

We went out the way we'd come in, through the window but not until I'd found a panel of switches and pressed one to open the main gates. Hoisting Terita Montez over a ten-foot wall wasn't something I fancied attempting and it wasn't safe to leave her behind.

The drive wound down between smooth green lawns uninterrupted by weeds or even bird droppings. The message must have got around even to Old Mother Nature that Corelli wasn't a man to upset.

Three-quarters of the way down the drive we passed beneath the shade of a giant oak tree that must have been there since Adolph Zukor was a lad. It was a momentary respite from the baking heat of the sun. It didn't last, the inside of the lieutenant's car was oven-hot. Air-conditioning, all the windows down and the fact that she was bending the speed limit to destruction wasn't enough to cool us off. Terita Montez didn't care, she lay on the back seat, mouth open, breathing heavy fumes over us.

We were speeding north on Sepulveda, neither of us speaking which in my case was because I was mentally hammering recalcitrant jigsaw puzzle pieces in with the heel of my shoe when the lieutenant suddenly hit the steering wheel hard with the flat of her hand.

'Oh, shit,' she said.

'What now?'

'Mullany and Carling.'

'What about them?'

'I fixed it for them to be out of the way for a while.'

'So?'

'So I had 'em seconded to airport security at Van Nuys.'

She took a left turn into Sherman Way and I could see the airport turn-off ahead. 'Never mind,' I told her. 'It's all part of life's rich, rotten tapestry.'

'Don't joke, Mace.'

I had Rafer Johnson's gun in my lap and was checking that everything was in working order. 'Who's joking?' I asked.

Chapter Twelve

Finding Roccisano was no problem. He was too fat to hide even at somewhere like LAX; on a small airport's concourse he stood out like a toad on a Ritz cracker.

He was in a corner munching on a sandwich, eyes lifted to study a TV screen that was imparting information.

We found another TV screen and tried to decide which snippet was most likely interesting the fat man. A private flight incoming from Philadelphia seemed most promising. It was due in ten minutes.

'Well?' I asked. 'How do we play this?'

'However we play it, I lose my badge.'

'Come on now, Lieutenant, if you were really worried about that you would've bowed out long ago.'

'Maybe, but I have a feeling this isn't the best way to play this. If we pick up Roccisano and Corelli we could be making trouble for someone.'

'Such as?'

'We still don't know where the Duke features in all of this, or why someone's been going around killing go-go dancers and shooting at you. In fact we know almost nothing even if we do have more information than we know what to do with.'

She was right but knowing that was so didn't help much.

I decided to walk over to one of the enquiry desks and discover as much as I could about the flight from Philly. I told the lieutenant and left her watching Roccisano who had now moved on to consuming a bagful of doughnuts.

I didn't learn much, just that the aircraft was owned by an LA-based charter company and had been rented for the round trip, LA to Philly and was now on its way back again.

I was walking back to the lieutenant when a man in police uniform rounded a magazine rack and froze on the spot facing me. It was Officer Mullany. His head snapped around from me to the far wall where Roccisano waited. As his head came back towards me he was unbuttoning the flap over his revolver.

I reached for Rafer Johnson's gun, hoping it wouldn't come to a fight. The airport wasn't busy, but neither was it empty of people.

'Don't do it, Mullany,' I yelled.

Behind him I saw Roccisano look around. Someone close to me on the left started screaming. I jammed the gun back in my pocket and took off in a low dive aiming towards Mullany's legs.

He scrambled to one side avoiding all but one outstretched hand. The movement unbalanced him and he crashed into the rack of magazines sending it spinning sideways, its contents flapping lazily through the air.

Mullany had the gun out and I tried to grab it from him but he had recovered and punched me with one hand, catching me squarely in the chest, while bringing the gun up with the other.

I heard footsteps running and the lieutenant's voice calling his name. Mullany began to squeeze the trigger.

I heard the shot and wondered why I wasn't hurting but then saw blood spraying from the back of his head. His gun dropped limply, then fell from nerveless fingers. I picked it up, scrambling to my feet as I did so.

Lieutenant Bercovici was walking towards me, her gun hand hanging straight down by her side, her eyes fixed on Mullany. Her shot had hit him in the face.

All around us people were lying on the floor, surprisingly not many were making much noise.

I couldn't see Roccisano.

I started towards where he'd last been standing and then saw him coming out of an office. He was moving quickly, a gun in his hand. I went after him, shouting his name. He turned and fired without taking time to aim. The bullet whistled harmlessly over my head. I dropped to my knees, aimed and fired. He crashed over like a punctured dirigible.

More footsteps, running.

I looked around and saw two men in uniform. One of them was Officer Carling. He recognised me and skidded to a halt. He looked from me to Roccisano, then across to where Lieutenant Bercovici was still standing over Mullany's body. Carling's companion was looking very dangerous but Carling spoke to him quietly. I didn't hear the words but the effect was clear. The other cop lowered his gun and we all looked at one another.

After a moment I climbed to my feet, walked over to Carling and held out my hand. He placed his revolver in it. His colleague was looking at all this blankly. I handed the gun to him. He took it hesitantly.

The lieutenant was walking towards us now, her gun no longer in view, her face set, her eyes straight ahead of her and avoiding mine.

I turned away and walked quickly to Roccisano's side. He was breathing through a fine mist of blood and saliva. 'Can you hear me?' I asked.

His eyes flickered towards mine.

'Who killed Maria and Ella?' I asked.

He tried speaking but all that happened was a curious whistling sound and a dribble of blood that ran down his chin.

I tried again, this time giving him questions he didn't need to answer with words.

'Did you kill Maria?' I asked.

His head moved fractionally to the side. No.

'Did you kill Ella?'

Another movement, this time vertically. Yes. I remembered Ella's young face and the bruises and the marks around her neck and I didn't feel so bad that the fat man was dying.

'Where is Vernon Duke?' I asked.

No movement.

'Is he dead?'

No.

'Is he a prisoner?'

A bubble of air caught in Roccisano's throat and he coughed. I tried to think of some way to ask a question about the strip of video film that could be answered either yes or no. I didn't succeed. The fat man's breathing was growing shallower. There wasn't much time.

'Where do I look?' I asked. 'Philly?' No. 'Terita's house?' No. 'McQuaid's house?' No. 'Corelli's house?' This time nothing, not a movement. 'Is it at Corelli's house?' I asked, not knowing what the hell "it" was. Again nothing came from the fat man. Then I realised that he had stopped breathing. Roccisano was dead.

I sat back on my heels.

I was conscious that someone was standing beside me. It was the lieutenant. I climbed to my feet and looked at her. For the first time since I'd met her nothing illuminated her eyes. They were flat and dull and without expression.

I remembered what I'd said to her last night after she'd

killed Rafer Johnson. 'I told you it didn't get any easier, didn't I.'

She looked down at Roccisano. 'Did he tell you anything?'

'He killed Ella. I think that's all.' I suddenly remembered the incoming aircraft, and the fact that when the shooting started Roccisano had taken time to go into one of the airport's offices.

I walked across to the door he'd come out of. A tousle-haired young man stood in the opening oblivious to the ringing of several telephones in the room behind him.

'What did he want?' I asked.

He swallowed nervously. 'He told me to call an incoming flight and warn the pilot there was trouble here. I could hear shooting and people screaming. I thought there must be someone important on the aircraft.'

'So you called it?'

'I called the tower, they called the flight.'

'Where's it gone?'

He shook his head. I thought about asking the tower but decided not to bother. Corelli would be covering his trail too well for that to be anything but a waste of time and effort.

The lieutenant was talking to Carling when I rejoined her. I stood to one side, half-listening, worrying over other things.

It wasn't Carling's fault, I gathered. It was all down to Mullany. A few easy bucks to keep Terita Montez free from interference. Taking me to the hospital had been part of that deal. He didn't know anyone planned to kill me, I was just to be kept out of the way for a few days.

He was probably telling the truth. I didn't think Terita knew about the killings, not at first. Nothing she'd done warranted murder. I counted up the bodies. Ella, Maria,

Leo Collis, Rafer Johnson, and now Officer Mullany and the fat man. It was too many by far.

It took quite a while to get away from Van Nuys airport. The local cops swarmed around asking all sorts of questions and Lieutenant Bercovici had to talk long and earnestly to her chief on the phone before he pulled strings and we were cut loose.

Part of the deal was that she would go straight back to his office and explain just what the hell was going on. She had to go direct, not via anyplace else.

We drove back along Sepulveda and when I saw a car rental sign and I told her to pull over and leave me there.

'I think the chief wants to talk to you as well,' she said.

'Later.' I looked at her and smiled, failing to get any response. Glancing around at Terita who was still snoring peacefully on the back seat I tried putting some of the odds and ends into order. 'Look, you can keep him happy on what we have. Or unhappy as the case may be, but you can certainly keep him busy. We have a porno movie maker with a couple of cops taking protection, we have a Philadelphia hit man, plus another couple of racketeers of some kind from the same place and we have some kind of plot against Vernon Duke. There's enough there to keep him busy for a month.'

'But we don't know what any of it means, or most of it.'

'We know that what started all this happened last Monday night at Terita Montez's house and that everything else stems from there. And that Linda Martin is still missing and may have the answer. Dammit, she must have the answer. All this killing isn't because somebody likes the smell of blood.'

She shivered and I placed my hand on her knee, squeezing gently. 'How many more have to die?' she asked.

‘Maybe that part of it’s all over,’ I said. I don’t know if I convinced her, I certainly didn’t convince myself.

‘Where are you going?’ she asked.

‘Back to Corelli’s house. Roccisano was trying to answer questions but when I mentioned Corelli he didn’t try yes and he didn’t try no. Even when he knew he was dying he wouldn’t rat on his boss. Dammit, he even made sure the plane wouldn’t land before he tried to make a run for it. My guess is that something is at Corelli’s.’

‘But what?’

‘I don’t know but one thing’s for sure, it isn’t something that can get up and walk away otherwise Corelli wouldn’t have taken a trip out of town leaving the place unprotected.’

‘I don’t know, Mace, all we seem to do is find more questions, never any answers.’

I leaned over and kissed her; she didn’t respond at first but at last it got through to her and I felt the tension drain out of her. ‘You saved my life again,’ I said.

‘At what cost?’

‘Forgive me if I don’t grieve over Mullany any more than I did over Rafer Johnson. Maybe I’m prejudiced but I think I’m more valuable than either of them.’

She pulled away slightly and looked very deep into my eyes. ‘I certainly hope so, Mace. If you’re not, it’s a price I’ll be paying for a long time to come.’

I climbed out and watched as she drove slowly away. Her last remark troubled me. I didn’t probe too deeply as to why because I had a feeling that the answer wasn’t one I would be happy with.

Half an hour later, with a car rented from a company that didn’t suspect I was fated to write off thousands of dollars worth of machinery just by signing my name to a slip of paper, I drove back to Bel Air and the house where we'd found Terita Montez drinking herself into an alcoholic stupor.

The gates were still unlocked thanks to my use of the electrics and I drove inside, carefully closing them behind me. I didn't want the local law, or anyone else for that matter, wondering what was happening at Corelli's mansion.

I drove past the old oak tree and parked the car around the side away from the eyes of anyone who came up the drive although I hoped that was a precaution I wouldn't need, then let myself in through the same window as before.

I was patient and I was systematic and it took hours to work my way through fourteen bedrooms, three with bathrooms, four additional bathrooms, a dining room big enough to feed the five thousand at one sitting, the study where Terita had done her drinking, a lounge big enough to house three four-seater couches, half a dozen club armchairs and a dozen or so assorted tables. I even made a search of the rooms outside adjoining the pool. The kitchen was a task all on its own, any gourmet working in there would have needed to gallop just to make one lap in the time it took an egg to boil.

Nothing.

Not a single solitary piece of anything that told me so much as the name of the man who lived here. It was the most impersonal house I have ever seen in my life.

I sat in the kitchen watching the day turn to night and scratched my head.

Then I remembered the hidden room at Terita's and went all around the house again, pacing out distances.

Nothing.

Thinking of Terita's hidden secrets brought me to the cellar beneath her studio. A house this size ought to have a basement area. A playroom, someplace to hide the booze.

It did. The way in was through a lift-up flap in the floorboards beneath the rug where the lieutenant and I had talked to Terita Montez.

It was large and dry and very cold. No games though, just rack upon rack of bottles of what turned out to be fine wine. Corelli hadn't struck me on our brief acquaintance as being a connoisseur of the better things in life but, then, I'd taken him for what he presented himself as – a punchy ex-prizefighter with a brain the size of a pea. I couldn't remember how many times I'd told junior detectives back home never to take anyone at face value. Certainly it was often enough not to have fallen into the same trap myself.

The only other things in the cellar were two large wooden cases, about four feet square and some five feet long. Both stood on pallets a few inches above the floor and in that space was coiled frosted white tubing. Refrigeration. That accounted for the cold.

I went up the stairs, through the house to the garage and eventually came back with a tyre lever.

The first crate was filled with magnums of champagne.

The second wasn't.

I stood looking down into the second crate for a long time, trying to work out what I'd stumbled into.

The body count had gone up by one.

It was a slightly-built figure, young, unmarked as far as I could see. Blond, straight hair, a well-shaped almost angelic face. A boy of about thirteen. Even in death, I recognised him.

He was the boy in the picture with Vernon Duke, candidate for Governor of the State of California.

After a while I reached in and gently turned the body over. I learned several things all at once.

I learned that he had died from multiple stab wounds in the back.

I learned that he had been subjected to a violent homosexual rape.

And I learned where the missing video had been hidden.

I took the video cassette out from beneath the body and lowered the boy back as gently as I'd lifted him. Then I went back upstairs and slotted the tape into a recording machine in the study, turned it and the TV on and sat down to watch.

It was like seeing a movie I had forgotten but in which I recognised each scene a fraction of a second before it appeared.

I was prepared for the setting, of course. The bedroom at Terita Montez's house with the one-way mirror serving the camera and now me as a peephole into a kind of hell.

Vernon Duke and the boy were there, sitting on the bed, actually looking at the camera only they were not seeing the camera. They were seeing themselves reflected in the mirror. A blond, smiling boy and the tanned, smiling, white-haired politician.

The camera zoomed in and took a head shot, the one I'd seen on the strip of tape Terita had found in Roccisano's pocket. Then it pulled back and absorbed the detail of the willing seduction that took place. The boy cooperated through the undressing and kissing and caressing.

He also cooperated through the mutual oral intercourse which followed.

It was the next stage where he began to resist.

At first it was just the smile that faded. Then something else came into the boy's eyes. Fear.

He struggled against it but the man was tough and fit

and easily overcame the boy's efforts. From somewhere on the floor Vernon Duke picked up strips of cloth. He used them to tie the boys hands to the head of the bed and his feet, legs spread apart, to the bottom of the bed.

Duke's expression was purposeful, his movements efficient.

I turned off the machine and went over to the bottles Terita Montez had used to such good effect. I poured myself a very large shot and drank it down in one gulp.

Then I went back to the set. I didn't want to see the rest of it because by now I not only knew each scene, I also knew how it ended. There was no 7th Cavalry waiting behind the hill to come to the rescue. This wasn't that kind of movie.

I turned the set on.

The rape was as violent as I knew it had to be to account for the injuries I'd seen on the boy's body.

The fact that the film was silent somehow made it worse. The boy's mouth open and screaming with no sound coming from between his young lips was frightening in its pathetic hopelessness.

The man was still pumping viciously at the boy when he took a knife up from where it had obviously lain with the cloth strips.

He didn't stop what he was doing, he just began stabbing in time with his bodily movements.

By the time Duke reached his awful climax the boy had stopped his silent scream and the only movement he made was that caused by the weight of the man on top of him.

The final scene was another zoom to close up. This time there was only one face in the frame, Vernon Duke. It was even smiling; a hideous, satiated grin that I knew I would not forget however hard I tried.

I stood up, turned off the TV and rewound the tape. Then I turned off the recorder, took the cassette out and stood with it in my hand.

'Pretty good, isn't it,' a voice said.

Corelli was standing in the doorway, his thick, fighter's eyebrows turning his grin into a killer's grimace. He had a gun in his hand. I'd lost count of how many people had pointed guns at me in the past week. I was tired of it; I was tired of all of it.

Corelli came a few paces into the room, his eyes raking sideways to check that I was alone.

'Put it down,' he said.

I put the tape down on top of the TV.

'The gun, too,' he said, gesturing at the bulge in my jacket.

I put the gun on top of the tape.

'Too bad you got mixed up in this,' he said.

'Too bad.' I agreed.

'Did you find that English girl?' he asked. The question didn't sound casual. He really wanted to know.

I shook my head and that disappointed him.

'What happened at the airport?' he asked.

'Roccisano's dead. So is Mullany.'

'Mullany?'

'One of the cops on the take from Terita.'

'Oh, him.' He didn't care for trivialities like dead cops. 'Did you kill Rocco?' he enquired.

'Yes.'

'How about Rafer?'

'No, somebody else got him.'

He shook his head slowly, his overcast eyebrows hiding any expression his eyes might have held. 'You've made some bad enemies, Mace.'

I shrugged.

'It never was any of your business,' he continued.

'Somebody made it mine.'

'Cops!' He made it sound like a dirty word.

I wanted to relax him; somehow I had to even the odds a little now that he had a gun and I didn't. 'What happened between you and Clara, back in the old days?'

Now it was his turn to shrug. 'She came home to Philly to promote a movie. She got pregnant.'

'Did she really kill the baby?'

'She'll do anything when she needs a fix.'

'A fix?'

'Heroin.'

'Then?'

'From when she was sixteen. All the pills and stuff the studio had her on started it. I supplied her supplier. When she came back to Philly we had to deal direct.' An odd light gleamed in his eyes. 'I always did go for women who . . .' He broke off and the gleam faded. He wasn't about to reveal his sexual proclivities to me.

'Is that why she helped you kill Maria, for a fix?'

He laughed. It sounded as bright and cheerful as a bad impression of Dwight Frye. 'Smart of you, Mace. Yes, she helped. That Mexican kid sure held out. I burned her but she didn't talk. Clara needed a boost so bad I told her to try.' He shook his head. 'She went too far, like with the baby. I never would've believed so much blood would come from a pair of tits.'

I wanted to kill him then.

It was such a powerful feeling that I was shaken by it. I had always held the belief that getting tough was something I could detach myself from. Something to turn on when I went on duty and to turn off again when the hands of the clock had moved through a normal working shift.

At that moment I knew that I was capable of doing the kind of thing the people I was supposed to fight against did every day. It was not a comforting thought.

Corelli must have read what I was thinking in my eyes. 'Don't try it,' he warned.

I couldn't read his eyes as we looked at one another. I didn't care that he knew what I wanted to do to him.

'A pity you found all this,' he said. 'I had in mind you might be useful . . .' He stopped again. More thoughts he didn't want to show.

I realised that I wasn't helping myself. I wanted him relaxed, not alert to anything I might try.

He moved from the doorway, crossing towards the TV set on which the cassettte and my gun stood, effectively making my task of getting out of there in one piece considerably more difficult.

Corelli appeared to be worrying over something. So far as I could see the odds were stacked on his side. Maybe I had missed out somewhere along the way. I replayed in my mind everything he'd said. Nothing leaped out at me.

He drummed his fingers on the TV set, his eyes on me.

'So, you don't know where the English kid is,' he said.

It really was worrying him and now it began to worry me. 'What's the deal?' I asked, indicating the cassette. 'Blackmail?'

He nodded. 'Something like that.'

'Don't tell me, let me guess. Your pal Rocco lucked onto a racket he could bend to set up some blackmailing deals. When you heard about it you got bigger ideas. You and your other buddy, McQuaid.'

He raised his scarred eyebrows. 'You figured that out too? Very smart of you, Mace.'

'You wanted something on Vernon Duke, something so big that he would do anything you asked him for, anything at all. With the State Governor in your pocket you'd be a big man, Corelli. So big all your friends back home in Philadelphia would eat out of your hand. And who knows, maybe after Governor he would move on to bigger things. One movie star already made it from this state to the White House, maybe another one would do the same. A different kind of star in a different kind of movie maybe, but think of the position that would put you in. The President of the United States in the pocket of the Syndicate. And you the man with the evidence.'

Corelli nodded agreeably. 'Pretty good, you have to admit,' he said.

'So now what?'

'Now you take a little ride, Mace.'

I suppose someone had to say that to me, sooner or later. After all, this is Hollywood. 'Of course, I'm not the only one who knows,' I told him.

He thought about that for a while although he didn't seem too worried. 'That female cop, you mean,' he said eventually. 'I don't think she'll give me any trouble. Just one call high up and she's out on her ear and if she squawks to the press, well . . .' He hefted the gun in his hand.

He was right. Lieutenant Bercovici wouldn't stand a prayer, least of all now when she was already on the carpet for breaking just about every rule in the book.

'So, I think we should take that ride,' Corelli said. He walked over to the flap leading to the cellar and glanced down, obviously thinking about the other refrigerated crate. Then he flicked the flap shut and pushed the rug over it. 'Someplace else, I think,' he said. He picked up the cassette and gun from off the TV and pointed at the doorway.

I went out and let him instruct me towards the back of the house. Another car stood behind mine. A large, dark blue limousine. 'Coming out of the closet?' I asked. 'What will people think if they see a bartender from Coliseum Street in a heap like that?'

He grinned as he opened the door for me. 'I'll tell them

I'm driving it for my boss. Anyway, people never notice bartenders, they're just people that serve drinks.'

He was right. Playing at tending bar in his own sleazy dive was the best cover he could have had.

'You drive,' he said.

I slid in behind the wheel and started the motor with the keys he handed me after he'd climbed into the back seat.

I drove slowly and carefully, the former to give me time to think, the latter so as not to jolt his gun hand.

We were whispering along Beverly Glen Boulevard, heading north when I noticed a car following us. It was too dark to be sure but it looked the same make as Lieutenant Bercovici's.

'Faster,' Corelli said.

I glanced at him in the rear-view mirror. He looked relaxed. I didn't think he had seen the other car. He had his gun resting comfortably across his forearm and pointing at the back of the seat I was in.

Ahead was the narrow place where I'd let the white Rolls-Royce come through. As if summoned up by some replay mechanism in my mind the same car was there again. The hood was up but I recognised the white-blonde hair in my headlights.

I pulled to one side and turned my head as if watching the driver as she floated past. In reality I was checking the whereabouts of the other gun. With the cassette it rested on the seat beside Corelli.

The other car was now tucked in tight behind me. As I looked ahead again I glanced into the mirror. The other driver flicked the interior light on and off again. It was Lieutenant Bercovici.

I moved off, picking up speed again to keep Corelli content but not so much so that the lieutenant would have any difficulty keeping in touch.

Corelli murmured directions from time to time and I

realised we were following the same path as that I had taken the night Mullany and Carling forced me off the road. It seemed like too good a chance to miss a repeat performance.

I picked up speed, not too noticeably, until we were going fast enough for what I had in mind and too fast for Corelli to risk shooting me.

Eventually he noticed. 'Take it easy, Mace. Got a death wish, have you?' He laughed at his own joke.

I flicked the wheel right and then left and the car jinked enough to rock Corelli in the wide expanse of the back seat.

I pulled hard at the wheel, then let go, opening the door with one hand while I rammed straight fingers into Corelli's face. Then, as he threw himself sideways I scrabbled for the cassette. I felt the case and the gun and snatched them up, I hurled myself sideways out through the open door as Corelli let go one shot. Something plucked at my sleeve and the things I was holding fell from my grasp.

Then I was out of the car and rolling over and over on grass and the car was heading faster down the slope.

The repeat performance was almost identical except this time there was no explosion.

Above me on the road the lieutenant's car slid to a halt and I heard her calling my name. Then, from the crashed limo a shot was fired and all hell broke loose.

The lieutenant loosed off four, maybe more shots very fast and then the replay was complete. One of her bullets hit the fuel tank of the big car and it went up in a sheet of flame.

In the sudden flash of brilliant light I saw Corelli running down the slope beyond the burning car. He reached a knot of people coming out to see what had disturbed their evening a second time.

'Are you okay?'

I turned to see the lieutenant standing beside me. 'I'll survive,' I said.

I began searching the ground.

'What are you looking for?'

I told her.

She brought a flashlight from her car and with that and the glare from the blazing limousine we looked for the cassette. We didn't find it. We did find the gun.

We didn't waste time looking for Corelli. He was out of reach. For the moment.

I thought about what had happened in the few moments before I'd flung myself from the crashing car. I'd had the gun and the cassette and I'd dropped them both. The gun we'd found so it had fallen clear of the car, the cassette we hadn't so it must have gone up with the bang. There was no way Corelli could have taken it.

For some reason, as the lieutenant and I drove away from the scene and I wearily began bringing her up to date with what had happened, I didn't feel as happy as I thought I should.

Chapter Thirteen

She didn't want to believe me, which wasn't really surprising because I didn't want to believe me either. But she did because there was no reason for me to lie and I believed it because I'd seen the film and I'd seen the body and I'd talked to Corelli.

'It makes a kind of sense of everything, I suppose,' she said eventually.

We were sitting in a bar off Sunset, thankful for the impenetrable gloom inside and aware of the determined glitter of the street outside.

'If the Syndicate hoped to fix a state governor, a man who might one day be President, then half a dozen dead people would be a small price to pay.' She sipped moodily at her drink.

'Except that the people paying that price were innocent, they just happened to be in the wrong place at the wrong time.'

'Maybe none of us is innocent,' she said. 'Not if we let our society turn out this way.'

I looked at her carefully in the dim light. Her expression was serious, as usual, but her tone was bleaker than I'd heard before. 'That's why we're police officers,' I said, trying for a lightness I didn't feel.

'Were,' she said. 'Past tense. I'm on suspension.' She finished the rest of her drink and waved for the attention of a bargirl who swayed over on four-inch heels and angled a fish-net covered hip towards my left ear while she took our order.

'Why?' I asked.

'Isn't that obvious? The rules that have been broken in the past few days include just about everything up to and including the greatest policeman's sin of all, encroaching on other division's territory. San Bernardino want my hide, Beverly Hills want it, three other divisions of the LAPD want it . . .'

'I want it,' I put in. 'But for different reasons.'

'Don't joke, Mace.'

'Who's joking?'

She glared at me, then her face muscles relaxed and she permitted herself the tiniest glimmer of a smile. 'Sorry, I'm letting it get on top of me.'

'Speaking of which . . .'

'Mace!'

I leaned forward and kissed the tip of her nose. 'Let me try another question. How?'

'How what?'

'How have they all homed in onto you, all these various departments?'

'There've been reports on the hour every hour, since you rode into town. A onc-man crime wave, the chief called it.'

'Me?'

'You haven't been keeping a low profile, have you?'

'Maybe not, but the fact that all this is being tied up in a neat package suggests that someone somewhere is piecing together everything that's happened and coming up with some of the right conclusions.'

'What do you mean?'

'I don't know, it's just that I have an uneasy feeling that for all these people to jump on you at one time, and for me to become the object of similar attention suggests some high level interest.'

Our drinks arrived. Looking up at the girl in the fish-net tights I saw that beneath the quarter-inch of panstick was the face of a girl who shouldn't have been out of school. She smiled at me, bright enough to light up a small town. I tried to imagine what she would be doing five years from now. Everthing I thought of depressed me still further.

'Look,' I said to the lieutenant after the girl had teetered away, 'if everyone knows what I've been up to, why haven't I been busted?'

She frowned at the question.

'If I'm in someone's hair, why haven't the police taken me out of circulation the way Corelli tried to do?'

'Are you suggesting someone wants you out here raising all kinds of hell?'

'I don't know what I'm suggesting but suppose we take advantage of two very important facts. One, whatever I've done I'm free to roam and plunder; two, now you're on suspension you're free of boring things like keeping up with the paperwork.'

'And how do we take advantage?'

'By treading on some very important toes.'

'Whose have you in mind?'

'Vernon Duke's, who else?'

'Without the cassette what can you do?'

'Not as much as I could do with it, but that's no reason not to try frightening him.'

She stared at her drink, then abruptly pushed it away and stood up. 'Okay,' she said. 'Let's go now before I think of the implications and get cold feet.'

'Don't worry, I have a cure for that, too, or have you forgotten already?'

She walked out of the bar, straightbacked, not letting me see her expression. I dropped some bills onto the table and followed.

'How come you still have your gun?' I asked as I caught up with her outside. 'In all the movies I've seen, suspension includes handing in gun and badge.'

'The gun's my own,' she said.

'And the badge?'

'They took that.' She stopped as we reached her car. Glancing across the roof at me, she smiled. 'To be precise, they took one of them.'

'Tut, tut, lieutenant, you're starting to think like me.'

'Then God help me.' She opened the door, climbed in and unlocked a door for me. 'I could do to go home and change first,' she said.

She was still wearing the black outfit and I had to admit that her customary elegance was showing minor signs of encroachment from the hassles of the past hours. 'Nice idea,' I said, 'but I have a feeling we might find ourselves being sidetracked.'

She started the car and moved out into the traffic. 'Maybe you're right,' she said. 'By the way, I called Barbara at the house. She sounded restless. Do you think she's safe now?'

'I hope so.'

I remembered the way Corelli had seemed interested in where Linda was, even at this late stage. I had an uneasy feeling that the troubles hounding the dancers from The Blue Whale were not yet over.

Vernon Duke's home was north of San Fernando perched high on a crest overlooking the Pacoima Reservoir. Eucalyptus trees formed a first line of defence, then a wall with closed-circuit TV cameras every few yards, two dog patrols and a team of private security men whose collected weaponry would have kept a

Central American republic in ferment for a year.

There was no way we were going in without permission.

Surprisingly, we got it.

I gave our names to a thick-necked individual at the main gate who looked us over with the eyes of a non-believer, then talked with someone on a telephone, then came back to look us over once more in the glare of the floodlights.

'Leave the car outside,' he said. 'And I'll take any weapons you have, you can collect them on the way out.'

He said that in a way that suggested that getting out would be considerably trickier than getting in.

We did as we were told and a jeep came down from the house to collect us.

The house was plantation-style with bits borrowed from Greece and even India. The architect must have been psychotic.

At the door, which is a poor word to describe an entrance through which an ancient emperor would have been happy to pass on his way to his coronation, stood a man in a black silk suit.

'McQuaid,' the lieutenant said as the jeep rolled to a smooth standstill.

I looked at the man as we climbed the steps towards him. He was medium height, chunky, and had the kind of face that sold ice-boxes to Eskimos. He was so sincere you could have chipped bits off him and sold them as good luck charms.

We told him we wanted to speak to his boss and he smiled brightly and said that wasn't possible because Vernon Duke was busy and, anyway, who said he was even here.

'We know about Corelli's game,' I said.

'Corelli?' His smile was even brighter. 'I don't believe I

know anyone of that name. All the politicians around here are well known to me. Perhaps he isn't a politician.'

'He's a hoodlum from Philadelphia.'

'Now, why would a man like that have any dealings with us?' he asked.

'Corelli can't finish his business, McQuaid. The evidence has gone up in smoke.'

'What business? What evidence? Gone up in smoke? You talk in riddles, Mr Mace.' He wasn't at all uncomfortable and we hadn't moved from the steps outside the door. I had an uneasy feeling that we wouldn't get past this point, added to which McQuaid was just too confident. He turned his bright smile onto the lieutenant. 'I've heard a lot about you, Lieutenant Bercovici,' he said. 'Even to the unfortunate fact that you appear to spend more time outside your area of jurisdiction than inside. As for your unfortunate suspension, well, someone with your . . . qualifications shouldn't have too much difficulty finding more congenial work.' He turned back to me. 'As for you, Mr Mace, you'll be going home soon, won't you? After you've located that unfortunate young lady, of course.'

He knew everything about us, and he didn't care if we knew that he knew. His confidence was more than that of a professional salesman. McQuaid really believed we were helpless and that whatever game he and Corelli were playing was far from over.

I turned away and started down the steps towards the waiting jeep, hearing the lieutenant follow me.

'If you have trouble getting work, Lieutenant,' McQuaid called, 'come and see me. Your qualifications have a certain appeal.'

I turned but she stopped me with a hand to my arm. 'Leave it, he has the power on his side.' She nodded her head towards the jeep. Glancing over my shoulder I saw that the driver was looking at me, a sub-machine gun resting on the back of the seat. If I took one step towards McQuaid he would cut me in half.

Neither of us spoke again, not during the long ride back down to the gate, not as we collected our guns from the man on the gate, not as we drove the first twenty miles of our journey back to the city.

'Don't let it eat at you,' the lieutenant said as we were passing over Chandler Boulevard.

I looked down at the road beneath the freeway and wondered how Marlowe would have handled this business. Probably much easier than I was managing, and with fewer dead bodies.

'He was too confident,' I said. 'And he knows too much.'

'McQuaid?'

'Yes. Obviously he's talked with Corelli since we saw him last and as far as they're concerned, the game's still on.'

'By now Corelli will have the boy's body hidden away.'

'The body doesn't help. It's the video that ties in Vernon Duke.'

'But that burned up in the fire.'

'That one did. What if there's a copy?'

'Would Corelli risk that? Keeping copies around might be an even greater risk than holding on to only one.'

'That isn't what I'm thinking. What happened to Terita Montez?'

'Nothing. By the time I'd been chewed out there was nothing I could do to hold her in custody. Why?'

'Let's go calling.'

'Are you planning to tell me what this is all about or are you just going to sit there and grin?'

'I'm not grinning, Lieutenant, believe me. I think I

know why Corelli was so interested to know if I'd found Linda.'

She was curious to the point of bursting but I wouldn't tell her what was on my mind.

Terita Montez let us in without quibbling. She sounded as though she was still drunk when she spoke over the intercom but after the gates were opened and we had driven up to the house she came out looking decidedly more sober than when I'd last seen her.

'How's Clara?' I asked as she led us into the living room.

'She's improving.' She studied my face carefully. 'What will happen to her?'

'I don't know but something tells me she'll be locked up for quite a while. As for Corelli, with luck he won't bother her again.'

'He's dead?'

I shook my head. 'But he's desperate and I think I know why. That why we're here. Let's go upstairs.'

She looked from me to the lieutenant and back again. Then she turned and led the way up. I took the key from the bedroom, then went into the darkroom and opened up the door into the secret room. Terita Montez watched me as if I was Frank Morgan doing his Wizard of Oz number.

The room was exactly as I'd left it. 'Is this how it always is when you were filming?' I asked.

She looked around. 'Yes, I guess so. No, that's not mine.' She pointed at the second of the two recorders, oddly tense.

I checked the connections.

I looked up at Lieutenant Bercovici who was watching me with as much curiosity as Terita was displaying, although with an undercurrent of mild irritation.

I let her seethe until we'd said goodbye to an edgy Terita and were back in the car again. It was turning light in the east as we drove up the road.

'Where to now, Mr Detective?'

'Home.'

'Home?'

'Your place. I want to make a phone call, it's time we saw that Barbara is okay, you need to change, I need a shave, and you want an explanation.'

'Thanks a bunch,' she said sourly.

'Okay, it's no big deal. That double recorder set-up meant there were two cassettes made at the same time. I should have known from the moment I saw the film at Corelli's. There were no hiccups in the film, no cuts, nothing. But Roccisano had a small piece of tape cut from the beginning of the film. It wasn't cut from the version I watched so there must be another.'

'Then where is it?'

I didn't like the answer but I couldn't think of any other reason for the deadly enthusiasm with which the girls from The Blue Whale had been hunted down and why Corelli was so keen to know if I was still looking for Linda. 'Linda's got it,' I said.

'Why?'

'I don't know why, but there can't be any other reason why they're still after her.'

Then a nagging thought began to nibble at the back of my mind. It wouldn't come into the open however hard I tried but I had the uneasy feeling that I was missing something.

'Why did Roccisano cut a piece from the tape?' the lieutenant asked, interrupting my thoughts.

'I don't know, unless he wanted something he could use in case Corelli decided he was surplus to requirements at any time.'

We had reached the house in Pandora Avenue and the lieutenant opened up and went straight through to the kitchen to start up the coffee. Then she went upstairs.

Moments later she was back down again.

'Barbara's gone,' she announced.

'Any sign that she went unwillingly?'

'No.'

'Maybe she just got tired of hanging around here. You said she sounded restive.'

'I hope so. If what you're guessing is right someone might try getting her to talk.'

'She doesn't know anything,' I said, uneasily aware that wasn't entirely true. I was equally well aware that Maria hadn't known anything either.

I reached for the telephone, scrabbling in my pockets for one particular telephone number.

Calling a jazz musician's home at around six o'clock in the morning isn't the kindest thing to do. Unfortunately, I had no choice.

A lady answered. I had never spoken to Bill Berry's wife Betty and I explained who I was and why I was calling. She sounded remarkably unruffled that some stranger was calling at such an ungodly hour and went off to wake her son, Bill Jr.

I asked him if he'd found anything for me about a rock musician named Gary.

He sounded surprised. 'Didn't you get my message?'

'What message?'

'I called the two numbers you left with Dad. On the second one the lady seemed to know what it was all about, so I told her.'

I read off the number on the lieutenant's phone and asked him if that was the one he'd given the message to. He said it was. At least I knew why Barbara had taken off. I asked him to tell me what he'd found out.

'A guy named Gary Paich, plays lead guitar and sings with a group named Windwalker. He's tall, blond and has an English girlfriend.'

'Perfect,' I said. 'Where can I find him?'

'He hasn't been around his apartment for a few days and hasn't been in touch with the rest of the band, but his folks live over in Eagle Rock.'

'Thanks,' I said. 'How much of this did you tell the lady you spoke to?'

'All of it. That was okay, wasn't it?'

I hoped so but I had an uneasy feeling that Barbara Collis might be getting back into the trouble I'd tried to keep her from. 'That's fine,' I assured him. 'Give my regards to your Dad and tell him I hope to see him soon.'

The lieutenant had gone upstairs while I spoke to Bill and now she was back wearing a pale grey smocked jacket over darker grey trousers which were tucked into calf-length soft leather boots. She had managed to tidy her hair and make-up and looked only sensational. I don't know how she did it. I felt half-dead and desperately needed a shower and the shave I'd promised myself. There wasn't time for either. There was only just time for coffee.

Traffic was building up and Santa Monica Boulevard was thick and slow but it still seemed the best way to go. I sat and fumed and worried over what Linda and now Barbara were letting themselves in for.

We were on the freeway, sweeping up in towards Glendale when the nagging worry at the back of my mind broke surface.

'I think I know why no one's arrested me and why you've been suspended in a way that would make you mad enough to keep on digging.'

'Why?'

'At first Corelli didn't want us around, that's why Rafer Johnson tried to kill me. Later, with Johnson dead and Roccisano doubtful and later still dead too, Corelli was short of foot soldiers. He needed to find Linda and he knew that I had as good a chance as anyone.'

'You mean he wants us to find her?'

I turned to look back down the road. We were leaving the Glendale Freeway to run into the centre of Eagle Rock. There were a few other vehicles making the same turn but I had no idea how long any of them had been behind us. 'I think so,' I said. 'He decided to let us help him look for her. When I found the boy's body he thought otherwise but not for long. He still wants me dead, I'm sure of that, but in his own time which means when I'm no longer any use to him.'

The lieutenant glanced up into the rear-view mirror. 'Maybe we should make a turn or two.'

'Don't make it too obvious.'

She glared at me. 'I'm not a beginner, Mace.'

I grinned at her and patted her knee which annoyed her even more but she didn't stay mad for long.

'I don't know whether I'll be glad to see you leave town or not,' she said.

For the first time I considered the truth of the fact that, one way or another, ten days from now I was due to take a flight out of San Francisco back to sunny Manchester. From there a short drive would put me back in Liverpool where my pint-sized and empty flat awaited my return. Empty save for a few books, some records, a creaky TV set and too many bottles of Scotch. Just now it didn't seem very much to go back to for reasons I didn't care to pursue but which increasingly centred on the beautiful woman beside me.

'I think you guessed wrong,' she said after a few minutes.

She was looking in her mirror again and I turned to check for myself. None of the cars that had come off the freeway behind us was still there.

'Maybe they're following Barbara,' I said. I hadn't asked what time Bill Jr. had called and spoken to Barbara but it had to have been last night. She had no means of getting out to Eagle Rock on her own, a cab would have been too expensive because she had little money, which left the bus. I checked the time. It was still short of eight o'clock. Hopefully she was still somewhere in transit.

We found a row of payphones and I went in to check the directory. There was only one Paich in Eagle Rock.

Ten minutes later we were on York Boulevard just behind the college and I was looking for the turning. Ahead of us, coming out of a main junction was a bus. I was half aware that the bus was stopping. The lieutenant was taking more interest and slowed to a crawl. I looked up to see what was interesting her.

She was watching people climb down from the bus. We were seventy yards short of the stop but even at that distance the tiny figure of the little black girl in her bright blue dress was unmistakable.

I had my hand on the door handle, ready to get out when the lieutenant grabbed my arm. We were stopped now. She pointed. A man had left the bus behind Barbara and was looking down the road behind him. A car, long, dark blue, slid into the curb. The man wandered casually over towards it and bent to speak to someone in the back seat.

The car was a match for the one that had exploded but, then, people like Corelli probably bought cars the way most people buy shoes, in pairs.

Barbara was looking for someplace on our side of the road and she was heading right towards us. I slid down in the seat, pulling the lieutenant down with me. A quick peek over the dash told me that Barbara had found what she was looking for. 52nd Avenue was ahead of us and she disappeared down it. The blue limousine floated after her at walking pace.

I grabbed the street map, desperately running my

finger along the road we were on. 'Back up,' I said.

She didn't need second telling and the tyres screeched as we hurtled in reverse along the street causing two oncoming drivers to have early-morning coronaries.

'Down there.'

We took off down a side turning that ran parallel to 52nd Avenue.

'Now right.'

Tyres howled.

'Left.'

Another protesting squeal.

'Right again.'

I hung on to the safety strap.

'Stop here.'

We ground to a standstill and I was out and running before the lieutenant had time to turn off the motor. I vaulted a low white picket fence, ran down someone's garden and scrambled up and over another, higher fence. Now I was in the gardens at the back of the houses on the west side of 52nd Avenue. Here the fences in between were wire stretched tight through concrete posts. I went over three gardens, trying to see something that might identify where I was in the street.

Then, through a gap between two houses, I saw Barbara Collis standing looking at a scrap of paper in her hand, then up at the house I was behind. She opened the gate and started up the path.

I ran up the garden, then, still three paces short of the back door, I launched myself feet first.

I rolled over backwards as I recoiled from hitting the door. There had been a satisfactory splintering crack from the timber, so I contravened recommendations and hit the door with my shoulder. The door burst inwards.

I was through the kitchen and into a narrow passageway as Barbara rang the bell.

Above me I heard voices, high-pitched and nervous. I glanced up the stairs. A tall young man with blond hair, naked except for a pair of black boxer shorts, was at the top looking down at me. There wasn't time for a discussion. I slipped the gun out of my pocket and showed him it.

He disappeared, fast as a jack rabbit.

I opened the door with my free hand and reached out to grab Barbara before she had time to speak.

Slamming the door shut I smiled at her, quieting anything she might try to say or do with a finger against her lips.

'Upstairs,' I said. 'And tell the others to stay there and keep quiet.'

Chapter Fourteen

There had to be at least three people to contend with. The man who'd got off the bus, the man he'd spoken to in the back of the limo and the driver. Unless they were idiots, which clearly they were not, one or more would go around to the back and see the havoc I'd wreaked on the door. Any advantage of surprise I might have had would be lost.

I unlatched the door and let it open an inch. It would look as if someone was careless. I hoped. I also knew that they wouldn't hang around for long. If Barbara was able to talk then the people in the house would make trouble, call the cops, yell for help, anything that would make difficult a task which should be easy.

With the encouragement of the open door, maybe they'd come in that way and do it quickly. Again I hoped.

Footsteps sounded on the path and paused at the door. Very slowly the door edged open another inch. A voice murmured something and more footsteps echoed as someone walked around to the back. I couldn't let him get there before I acted.

I tensed, ready to yank the door open but then the man outside showed impatience. And carelessness. The door opened wider, with me behind it.

A figure stepped inside and I hit him once, hard behind the ear. He went down with a bang that could've been heard in Pasadena. I hit him again to make sure.

From behind the house I heard a yell. A woman's voice. Then a shot, then another.

I opened the door and ran out into the garden at the front of the house.

The limousine was parked some yards down the block and I ran towards it, aware that I wasn't being very bright. The car's windows were tinted but I could make out a figure inside scrambling over from the back seat into the front. I stopped and let a shot go. The windscreen crazed.

Then the car was moving forwards, fast. I tried another shot as it went past me but it kept right on moving.

Down at the end of the street a school bus appeared and stopped, momentarily blocking the roadway. The big car skidded to a halt, then reversed back towards me. At that moment Lieutenant Bercovici appeared, running around the corner of the Paich house. She came out into the street as the dark blue limo swung backwards into an open driveway, then lurched forward in a fast, curving swing. It was headed straight for her.

I covered the gap faster than I've ever moved in my life before, taking off in a forward dive and grabbing her around the knees to carry her backwards through the neat white fence and onto the front lawn. I felt the wing of the car brush against my legs.

I managed one more shot as the big car rocked and rolled down the street before it turned into the main road at the end and vanished from sight.

I helped the lieutenant up to her feet and held her close.

'Thanks,' she said.

'Any time,' I assured her.

'Was that Corelli?'

I hadn't seen the man at the wheel too clearly but it

couldn't have been anyone else. I told her it was. We went around the back of the house. A thin-faced man was sitting on the ground nursing a shoulder from which blood was oozing. He was handcuffed to a rainwater pipe.

'Neat,' I said.

'I was aiming at his legs,' she said with a grin.

'Careful, you might get to like all this Dirty Harry stuff.'

'There's no fear of that happening.'

We took the wounded man inside and refastened him, this time cuffing his good wrist to the ankle of the man I'd slugged.

I looked up the stairs.

Three faces were looking down at me.

The young man I took to be Gary Paich, Barbara Collis, as wide-eyed and frightened as the first time I'd seen her, and behind them the pale face of Linda Martin.

'Am I glad to see you,' I said.

I went up the stairs and she pushed past the others meeting me halfway in an embrace that threatened to send us both backwards.

Downstairs I could hear the lieutenant dialling on the telephone. I couldn't imagine how she was going to explain this to the local police department.

We went into the bedroom.

I shook my head at Barbara. 'Why didn't you call me?' I asked.

'I didn't know how to reach you. I came out here in case I could help Linda. I wanted to . . . well, you were kind to me.'

Linda still had an arm around my waist that was threatening my circulation. 'And I didn't know how to reach you either,' she said.

'What happened at Terita's?' I asked.

'I don't know. It was a party, just like all the others

except that Terry wasn't there. Then, about one o'clock, Roccisano came down the stairs and said the party was over and we all had to go home. Ella had a package, I don't know where it came from.'

I heard the phone tinkle below and waited.

Lieutenant Bercovici came up the stairs and into the room. 'Okay?' I asked.

'About that job you offered me, directing traffic someplace, does it still hold good?'

I grinned. 'Listen,' I said. 'Your problems will soon be over. Go on,' I added to Linda.

'Ella and I took a cab. She got out at the house but I decided to keep the cab.' She held out a hand to Gary, relaxing her grip on me for the first time. 'Because it was early I thought I would go and hear Gary and the band. As I was getting out the package was still on the seat. Ella had forgotten it.'

A fatal slip of the memory. Leaving the package behind had cost Ella her life.

'I stayed at the apartment with Gary that night,' Linda continued. 'Next morning I remembered you were coming around and I went back to the house. There were police everywhere. I went back to Gary. Then I heard on TV that Ella was dead.' She shivered. 'Gary's people are away on vacation so he suggested we come out here until we could decide what to do.'

'Probably the best thing you could do,' I said.

'I suppose they're pretty angry with me at The Blue Whale,' she said to Barbara.

I looked at the tiny black girl and she looked at me. Something must have passed between us that communicated itself to Linda.

'What else has happened?' she asked.

I shook my head wearily. 'It's a long story,' I said.

'Have you spoken to my Dad?' Linda asked.

'Not yet.'

Outside, police sirens were coming closer.

'Maybe we . . .'

'There'll be time for that later. Have you the package?'

She reached under the bed and handed it to me. A brown padded envelope, just big enough to take a video cassette.

'Thanks,' I said as I jammed it into the pocket of my coat. Another piece of clothing was being ruined. I was getting quite good at it.

I went downstairs with Lieutenant Bercovici and sat patiently while she talked to a couple of faintly disbelieving detectives whose Eagle Rock calm was mildly disjointed by events.

Later, when things had relaxed a little, Linda called her father. Tearful promises were made about living the straight life from now on and that she would be home very soon.

The former was probably rooted in fear because I'd explained a little of what had happened to her dancing friends. I wasn't too sure about the other promise. Gary the guitar-player was holding her hand in a distinctly proprietory manner.

It was almost lunchtime before the lieutenant and I were able to leave. She was under strict orders following a telephone conversation with the Chief of Detectives in her division. She had to go there directly; no excursions, no delays, do not pass go, do not collect 200 dollars, just go directly to . . . I hoped not. In fact, she did say that he hadn't sounded quite as cranky as at their last meeting.

'He'll be even happier when I hand him the video,' she said as we began the drive back towards Hollywood.

'Not yet,' I said.

She snapped a quick glance at me as she negotiated her

way around a heavy trunk that was lumbering ahead of us. 'No more games, Mace.'

'It isn't that easy,' I told her.

'Why isn't it? All we have to do is hand the Chief the video and let the law take its course.'

I didn't want to argue with her but I had to because my plans were not the same as hers. Not by a long way.

I held up a hand and ticked off points. 'One, Corelli is still very much around; two, McQuaid still has the fix in and we don't know where. Without the boy's body even this video might not weaken it completely. Three; your Chief may be a big man in his division but he'll think very hard and carefully before going into the ring with the man who might be the state's next Governor.

'He'll do it.'

I had an uneasy feeling that the lieutenant was displaying an over-optimistic view of her own system's strengths and weaknesses. True, my version was rooted on the improbabilities of how I'd seen it happen on TV and in movies but I couldn't risk a Chief of Detectives I had never met against a potential State Governor. Admittedly, I hadn't met him either, not exactly, but I'd seen him on TV with the Vice-President so he had to carry most clout. If he didn't, he wouldn't be front-runner with backing from the White House. It seemed as simple as that.

'Maybe he will do it,' I said. I ticked off another point. 'Four, I will feel much happier when this video has been duplicated.'

'I promised I would go straight in and this time I think I should obey orders, otherwise I'll have no chance of reinstatement.'

'What was all that about a job in England?'

'Even if it was possible, I don't think it would be a very good idea.' She sounded sad about it.

I thought about it for almost five miles. 'You're probably right,' I said eventually. I sounded just as sad.

'What do I tell him?' she asked.

'The Chief? Tell him everything. Blackmail of Vernon Duke by Corelli who's hand in glove with Duke's own personal aide. Roccisano trying to siphon off some of the action for himself and killing Ella when he lost the package. Then he must have crawled back to Corelli and told him what had happened. Maybe he covered himself, saying he'd made a duplicate for safety and the girl had stolen it. My guess is that before she died Ella told him she'd left the package in the cab with Linda. That made Linda the number one target so Corelli took a personal hand, killing Maria in an attempt to make her talk, sending Rafer Johnson after me when I was getting too close, first in Watts then at the Meridian. Then, when things really hotted up he did what we guessed might happen. He decided to let us lead him to Linda only Barbara Collis did it for him.'

We drove on for a while longer.

'Okay,' the lieutenant said after she had obviously thought about it all. 'There's only one thing. Without the film there's no way the Chief will believe the hold Corelli has over Vernon Duke.'

She was right, of course. If I hadn't seen the film I don't suppose I would have believed it either. 'Just call it blackmail for reasons you'll be able to confirm when I bring the film in.'

She took her eyes off the road to look at me longer than was safe. 'I have to take it in, Mace.'

'How many times have you wrapped up a case so tight it was flameproof, waterproof, bombproof, everything-proof, only to see the prisoner walk out of the courtroom scot-free? Not because he was innocent or that you'd got it all wrong but because of some technicality, a legal nicety that had all the lawyers shaking hands with one another and smiling at a triumph for the law while justice wept out of blind-eyes.'

She looked at me curiously. 'I didn't have you down as another Harry Callahan,' she said.

'I'm not, at least I hope I'm not because he's just as bad. The only thing is, his way the bad guy's don't win.'

She didn't speak for some moments. Eventually, quietly, she asked. 'What do you want me to do?'

'I want time to stack the deck a little, just to give our side an even chance.'

'I must have the video.'

'You'll have it,' I promised.

'And you'll do nothing illegal?'

'Of course not,' I said with such conviction that I believed myself for almost ten minutes.

Chapter Fifteen

Lieutenant Bercovici dropped me off at the top of the road leading towards Vedado Avenue and I walked down to Terita Montez's house.

It was hot and muggy, the sun straining through an overhang of residual smog that made the atmosphere like that inside a hothouse. I was sweating by the time I reached the gate. She didn't answer the bell beside the gate so I went next door and rang Helen Jerome's bell instead. I had to go there anyway.

She was pleased to see me and in a way I was pleased to see her. I only wished it was time for me to make the promised social call but it wasn't, there were still things to be done.

I repaired the cassette, joining the two ends together where a piece had been snipped out. Helen wanted to do it for me but obscurely I didn't want her to handle it, not when I knew what the film depicted. I borrowed two blank tapes from her and then I went down to the bottom of Helen's garden and climbed over into Terita's.

She was lying beside the pool on a brightly coloured lounger. She opened her eyes and looked up at me. There was a bottle and a glass beside her on the edge of the pool. She was well away.

She tried to sit upright but the effort was too great. She had on the same yellow swimsuit she'd worn the first time I came here. It seemed like a quarter of a century ago.

'Roccisano's dead,' I told her. 'So is Officer Mullany. One or two other people are in custody and Corelli is on the run. By tonight, Vernon Duke will be off the hook. No one left to bribe or blackmail or otherwise chisel.'

'What crap are you giving me now, Mace?'

'Roccisano had a piece of video tape in his pocket, that's what you told me.'

She was looking at me, suddenly wary. I reached out and topped up her glass. She drank it convulsively. I topped it up again.

'If he had a copy, why would he have need for a dupe? You nearly threw me, telling me the second video recorder wasn't yours. But it was, the whole set up was too professional for a thug like Roccisano. For you, it was a piece of cake. You and Roccisano were partners in the blackmail racket, it wasn't his idea. Again, he wasn't smart enough.'

She emptied her glass again and once more I filled it.

'When Corelli told Roccisano that a special deal was coming down you wanted a piece of that action too. My guess is that you were here all along, hidden in the room upstairs. You took the film of Vernon Duke, making sure there were two copies. You knew Roccisano would take the spare copy with him so you needed an edge. You snipped a piece of tape out. From the beginning, the section where you carefully arranged to have both faces in close up. I guess you had a crazy idea you could pressure Corelli with it if your partner wouldn't play. This was way out of your league from the very beginning, Terita.'

She tried to get out of the lounger but she was too drunk. I filled the glass and watched as she swallowed more bourbon.

'What happened to the tapes of Linda and Ella?' I asked.

She would have told me anything by now. 'In Clara's room.'

'What were you looking for at Corelli's house?'

She stared at me, totally glassy-eyed now. I couldn't be sure if she understood what I was saying.

'The body, I suppose. What did you plan to do? Take another picture to add to your collection?' I shook my head at her naivety and emptied the rest of the bottle into her glass. She drank, slurping up the liquid and hanging onto the glass as if her life depended upon it. 'Just out of interest, who supplies Clara with heroin? You?'

She nodded sleepily.

'You bitch,' I said mildly. 'So you went to Maria's because you knew what Clara had done and wanted to be sure nothing tied the girl's death to Clara because that would have come too close to you. You didn't care about Clara, or Maria, or that boy. All you cared about was you.'

I stood up. She was breathing heavily, great gasping intakes of air. She was almost unconscious.

'You stood there with your camera and you watched that boy as he was raped and murdered and all you thought about was the money you could make. And I can't prove a word of it.'

She was snoring now although she wasn't asleep. She looked awful.

I leaned closer and put my lips close to her ear. 'How about a swim, Terry?'

She make a noise that could have been agreement.

'Go ahead, it will make you feel better.'

She began to struggle out of the lounger.

I went into the house, rigged up the two recorders and set them to work making copies of the video. While that was happening I searched Clara's room and found the master videos of the act that Linda and Ella performed for the sink-dwellers. I couldn't do anything about any copies in circulation, except hope that they wouldn't reach Liverpool, but at least there would be no more.

I glanced out of the window, down into the garden and the shimmering swimming-pool. Terita Montez had followed my suggestion.

When the copy of the death-video was ready I re-set the machines and repeated the process until I had four copies plus the original. It meant using up most of the videos lying around the place but it didn't matter to anyone, not now.

It was quite a while before I took all my videos downstairs and went into the garden.

Terita Montez had taken a dip in the pool but it hadn't refreshed her. All the booze I'd encouraged her to swallow had seen to that. She was floating, face down, and quite dead. I stood for a moment, looking at her body. The bright yellow of her swimsuit contrasted vividly with the unnatural turquoise brilliance of the waters of the pool.

I tried to feel regret but I couldn't fake that particular emotion. Instead, I wiped the empty bottle free of my fingerprints, then tossed it into the water beside the body. It gurgled softly as it filled and sank.

It was the only sound, it was that kind of afternoon.

I went back to Helen Jerome's because I needed a cab and didn't want to risk using Terita's phone.

Helen insisted that I could borrow her car, telling me it seldom was used and would benefit from a run out. She also asked me if I'd seen Terita Montez. I told her she was sitting by the pool and was very, very drunk. I also told her that she was aggressive and shouldn't be disturbed. I felt bad at lying to the old lady and at involving her in the way I was. I hoped that, if I could have told her what it was all about, she would have understood. I think she would have done so, she was that kind of woman.

Her car turned out to be a 1936 drop-head Bentley. It was beautiful and however inappropriate for what I had in mind, I took it gladly. I only hoped that my poor record with motor cars was over.

It wasn't the kind of car you drive too fast so it was late afternoon when I had made all my calls and headed out for San Fernando and Vernon Duke's mansion.

The floodlights were on, the guards patrolled, the dogs and their handlers all sneered at me.

The same thick-necked individual was on the gate. I told him to call McQuaid up on his phone and to let me talk to him. Just in case McQuaid was still playing it tough I told the guard to tell him I had the video. The guard looked at me as if I was crazy but it worked. I told McQuaid to let me in and no nonsense and that I didn't want to be searched. He told me to put the guard back on and moments later I was steaming gently up the slope in the Bentley, thinking how nice this place would be if it wasn't for the sweet smell of corruption that hung low over it like a funeral pall.

McQuaid was standing at the top of the steps again but as I walked up towards him some of the confidence was missing. He didn't look at my face, just at the package I had in my hand.

'Has Corelli called you recently?' I enquired.

'What's it to you?' he asked but the look in his eyes told me that Corelli had been too busy to keep him informed of recent events.

'Lieutenant Bercovici is talking to the Chief of Detectives about now,' I said. 'Among other things she'll tell him about Corelli and his people being responsible for at least three deaths. She'll also tell him about the body in

Corelli's cellar although I expect it's been moved by now. Shouldn't be at all surprised if she doesn't tell him about the mob from Philadelphia and how they planned to have their very own state governor and maybe even their own President of the United States. Of course, proving all this will be tricky, especially now that Roccisano is dead, and Officer Mullany and Terita Montez.'

The chances were that McQuaid wouldn't know the names of the smaller fry but the cumulative effect of the killings was working on him.

'Eight people are dead so far, McQuaid, and it all stems from you and Corelli. Now, like I said, proving it will be hard but tying you into Corelli will be easy. That's something else Lieutenant Bercovici will be telling them about, the landline between your house and Corelli's.'

All his confidence had gone now. He couldn't have sold a block of ice to a nomad in the desert.

'So, you'd best make tracks for wherever it is you think you can hide. But before you do that, I want to talk with Duke.'

'Why?'

'You can't keep him hidden away forever, McQuaid. The tale about assassination attempts won't help now. The law will want to see him, talk to him, question him.' I looked up at the big house and its impressive façade. 'Fancy place. Bought with his wife's money, I suppose. I expect she might want to ask him a few questions as well. She's from Philadelphia too, I hear.'

He nodded.

'What was her connection?'

He thought about not answering but it wasn't a secret worth keeping, not any more. 'When she was planning to marry him her father put an enquiry agency onto him. They turned up some interesting facts about his . . . personal habits.'

'He'd done it before?'

'Yes. Often.'

'Including killing?'

'Only once.'

He made it sound like a minor peccadillo. 'The same way?'

'Yes.'

So that was how they'd known to have strips of cloth and the knife ready. 'Why wasn't the marriage stopped?' I asked, but I'd guessed the answer.

'The agency making the enquiries was owned by Corelli's people.'

'So they sat on it, until it was of most use.' I looked at him, seeing only an image from the final moments of the video. I wanted to hit him but I asked a question instead. 'Where do you fit in? Are you from Philadelphia?'

'Me? No. I was . . . I heard it all from Corelli.'

'When he bought you.'

He shrugged carelessly without speaking. There was no need, money had done all the talking that was needed.

'Where's Vernon Duke's wife?' I asked.

'Florida. She always tries to keep a few thousand miles between them. A month before the election she'll show up, hold his hand, smile at the cameras, then go back.'

'She knows?'

'Not the details, just enough to stay away.'

'Hasn't she heard of divorce?'

He shook his head. 'Religious reasons.'

It sounded like a severe case of hypocrisy to me but I didn't say so. After what I'd done to Terita Montez, and knowing what I had planned for Vernon Duke I couldn't moralise.

It crossed my mind that perhaps, out of all this mess, Duke's wife might be the only one to actually benefit. It was a high price to pay for one woman's happiness.

I wondered if Lieutenant Bercovici had got around to the snippet about McQuaid's landline. Maybe it was time to nudge him homewards.

'Call Duke,' I told McQuaid. 'Tell him he has a visitor.'

He hesitated, looking at me as if searching for a clue to what I had in mind. He looked at the package again. He wanted to ask if that was why I'd said I didn't want to be searched but I was growing impatient.

'Call him,' I said.

He walked towards the door. When he heard me following he turned. 'Wait here,' he said.

'Don't be stupid, McQuaid. Now, do as you're told before I break you apart.'

His eyes darted nervously from side to side. He was looking for the hired help. It still hadn't fully sunk in that the game was over.

I jabbed him in the chest with stiff fingers. 'Move,' I said.

He thought about arguing but changed his mind. I followed him into the house through the giant doorway. Inside was a hallway into which a three-ring circus could have fitted with space left over for a freak show.

McQuaid's office was all red leather and mahogany and three-inch pile carpets. On the wall behind his eight-foot square desk were signed portraits of famous people. Very soon they would be denying McQuaid had ever existed.

He spoke into a rust-coloured telephone, appeared to argue, them put on some verbal pressure. Even at this late stage in the game McQuaid had pull with his employer.

'Down the hall,' he said. 'Last door on the left.'

I went to the door. 'Of course, if you were to pull out the landline you might be able to talk your way out of this,' I told him.

He stared at me in surprise, as if the man who'd just hit him with the custard pie was offering to mop up the mess.

I went out and down the hall to the last door on the left. I went in without knocking.

The room behind the door made McQuaid's office look like a slum. Crisp white carpets, blond-wood furniture, Scandinavian style, pale green couches and armchairs in a soft woollen fabric.

Despite the warmth of the evening a log fire was burning in the grate of a fireplace that was more Adam than Adam.

Standing with his back to the fire was the would-be Governor of California. He was wearing a light-grey, double-breasted suit that had been cut and tailored by an angel, a soft white shirt that gleamed, and a pink and grey-striped tie that had probably cost more than it would take to feed a family in Watts for a month. His shoes were handmade moccasin-style in tan pigskin. He looked good enough to vote for.

'McQuaid said this was important,' he said. His voice was pitched low but it carried well.

'Don't bullshit me, Governor,' I said. 'You're seeing me because McQuaid told you to and you do as McQuaid says.'

His colour heightened as blood flushed his tanned cheeks.

'And you do as Corelli tells you. How does it feel to be the lap-dog for a bunch of hoodlums who make their living out of drugs and gambling and other people's miseries.'

'Don't preach at me, godammit, he snapped, pulling fire from somewhere.

I walked towards him and he stepped to one side. I opened the package and slid out the cassette Linda had taken. He stared at it, hypnotised.

'Corelli lost the original, did he tell you that?'

From his expression it was obvious this was news.

'But there was a copy, this copy. Corelli has been looking for it ever since. Only I found it first.'

Something gleamed in his eyes, maybe it was the firelight but I didn't think so. 'How much do you want?' he asked.

'I've seen the film,' I said.

He straightened his back, trying to look down at me imperiously but he wasn't tall enough and he wasn't sure enough of himself.

'One hundred thousand dollars,' he said.

'What was the boy's name?' I asked.

He stared at me as if I'd gone crazy.

'The boy you raped and murdered, what was his name?'

'I don't know,' he said.

'Somehow, I didn't think you would. Nobody cared enough, I suppose. McQuaid told Corelli about your predilections, Corelli told Roccisano who told Terita Montez. Somewhere along the line a boy was procured. Roccisano and Montez watched you in action and made no attempt to stop you. But, then, they wouldn't, would they? It would have spoiled everything. The strips of cloth you used to bind the boy, the knife, all ready and waiting. They all knew what the outcome would be. It wasn't a murder, it was a sacrifice.'

'A quarter of a million,' he said, his voice thick.

'Is that the going rate for a young boy's life?'

'I told you, don't preach.'

'You know something? Even as I drove up here I had a faint hope that I might hear from someone, even from you, just a single word that suggested compassion for that kid, or for Ella or Maria.'

His eyes told me that not only did he not know the names of the two girls but that he wouldn't have cared a damn anyway.

I was holding the cassette loosely in my hand and he snatched at it suddenly, pushing me backwards. I didn't try to stop him, not even as he threw it on the fire. I stood and watched it flare up, then turned to smile at him.

He was looking at me triumphantly but the look changed when he saw that I didn't care.

'I had four copies of the video,' I told him. 'I delivered them before I came out here. One to your opponent at the election, one to the local office of the FBI, another I had sent over to the police by messenger because I didn't want to show my face there in case they tried to stop this visit. The fourth copy is with a lawyer who will give it back to me when I ask for it. If I don't show up in twenty-four hours, he will mail it to Washington to a man who will not have any doubts about how to treat you. Maybe I should have made another copy, for your wife.'

He was pale under the tan now; it made him look yellow.

'Why? Why, dammit? I would have paid you, paid anything.'

'I'm a stranger in this country, but I've read about your legal system. In some ways it's a lot like ours, in many more ways it's very different. One of the differences is that your judges are elected, which makes them bribable. Another difference is the way appeals can drag on for years, even for decades.'

I picked up the package from which I had taken the cassette and walked towards the door.

'After a few years, with your money and your past influence, the dust would have settled. You wouldn't have been executed for what you did. After all it was a film and everyone knows that films can be faked. That's why Corelli needed to keep the boy's body. I don't know if I could find that now and without it a good lawyer, and I've no doubt you can afford the very best, would get you off the worst charge. Who knows, with a few well-placed bribes he might even get you off all charges.'

I opened the door.

'This way, you're still hooked.' I held up the package. 'Of course, there's one way for you to get off the hook altogether.'

I placed the package carefully on a table by the door, went out and walked down the hall listening to the sound of my footsteps echoing into the silence. I seemed to have done that almost as often as I'd been hit on the head or had wrecked a motor car.

Outside I climbed into Helen Jerome's Bentley and sailed smoothly down to the gate.

'Mr McQuaid gone, has he?' I asked the guard.

He scowled at me, but his eyes were wary. I had pull and he was the type to respect people like that. 'Yeah, went out like his tail was on fire.'

'I suppose it was, in a manner of speaking.'

I looked back up towards the house wondering how long it would take Vernon Duke to decide what to do with the gun I had left in the package I'd placed on the table by the door.

When it came, the shot was surprisingly loud. The thick, warm silence of the evening was partly the reason, I suppose.

The guard stared up the slope towards the house.

'Sounds like trouble,' I said, and drove off into the darkness away from the floodlights and the guards and the dogs. Maybe it was my imagination but the air seemed to smell just a little bit sweeter.

Chapter Sixteen

I was in no great hurry to get back. Lieutenant Bercovici would be still tied up with the reports and statements and explanations and there was no one else I wanted to see. So I took the San Diego Freeway and dropped down into Santa Monica and took a look at Venice. There was no touch of evil about it, just a calm, soft, warm evening disturbed only by the clacking of rigging as the countless yachts swayed at their moorings.

I left Helen Jerome's Bentley and strolled for a while, thinking that although I'd seen more of Los Angeles than most Angelinos, I hadn't seen many of the places I'd planned to visit. Maybe there would be a chance now, and in very pleasant company.

On the way back to the car I slipped coins into a newspaper vendor and took a copy of the next day's *LA Times*. From the car I took the tapes of Linda and Ella, found a quiet corner and used the newspaper to start a fire. I hoped it might be one that would cleanse Linda's life, wherever she chose to spend it.

Back in the car I decided to go home in style. I took down the hood, turned on the radio and floated along Santa Monica Boulevard thinking how easy it would be to stay here, if I could afford the indulgence. And if the lieutenant proved agreeable. The radio was playing an old Dinah Washington tune; 'Look to the Rainbow', all saccharine lyrics and treacly strings with the voice cutting through like an unhoned razor and finding sadness amidst all the schmaltz. Somehow, it seemed appropriate and I didn't want to think too deeply about why.

I glanced upwards, beyond the honecombed concrete façades of stores and offices, towards the starlit sky. It was one of those nights when you can see from here to there and back again and every inch of the way is beautiful.

Despite the hour illuminated signs glowed, flashed and flickered in unequal contest with Old Ma Nature. Everything was on offer from ordinary hotels to those with adult movies and outsize waterbeds, from all-day breakfasts to car washes, from drive-in diners to all-night drugstores.

Liverpool would seem pretty dull after all this. Safer, undoubtedly but dull. It wouldn't just be the nightlife and neon; most of the dullness would be down to the absence of Lieutenant Bercovici.

One particular sign caught my eye. Anyone calling a Los Angeles bar, The Pub had to have a sense of humour so I stopped the car and went inside.

It was quiet to the point where the silence pressed against the eardrums. I was the only customer.

'We're closed,' a thin-faced man behind the bar counter said. He checked the time. 'Are you out late or making an early start?'

'Just a tourist,' I told him. 'Far from home and seduced by your sign.'

'Huh?'

'Why call it The Pub?'

'An Englishman helped me raise the money I needed to set it up. You're English, aren't you.'

I nodded.

'Maybe you know him. His name's Jackson, came from London.'

I suppose it's a habit Americans have acquired through thinking of England as a tiny tin-pot place. 'No, I don't think we ever met,' I said.

'Used to be called the Open Door,' he told me.

I remembered how Mundell Lowe, the guitar-player, would talk about a club he'd played in New Orleans when he was a youth. It too was called the Open Door, because it didn't have one. Someone had stolen it. I told the owner of The Pub and he laughed and told me his name and I told him mine. We were old friends very quickly. He seemed like a nice guy.

'How about coffee?' he asked. 'I could use one myself.'

'Thanks,' I said.

He went off through the back, reaching up to turn on a TV set as he did so. I didn't need entertaining and I was out of my seat and reaching for the off-button when I recognised the pictures on the screen. It was *Countess from Chicago* and there was Helen Jerome in all her young glory.

When Brad, the bar's owner, came back with two large mugs of coffee he joined me on my side of the counter. 'I love these old movies,' he told me. 'Beat the crap out of what they do today, *Jaws 10* or *Rocky 14* or whatever the hell is the latest box-office smash.'

I nodded.

'Take her,' he said, pointing up at the screen. 'They don't make 'em like Helen Jerome anymore.'

I looked at him more closely. He was about sixty, wiry, could have been a fighter once or some kind of sportsman.

'Come outside,' I said. 'There's something you might like to see.'

I showed him the Bentley, then reached inside for the licence and handed it to him. He read it in the light of a curbside payphone, straining against poor eyesight. 'Well

I'll be damned,' he said. 'Helen Jerome.' He shook his head, handing the licence back to me reverentially. 'You won't believe this,' he said. 'I met her once. I worked on a movie with her. I was stunting them. I took a fall from a moving car. The routine went wrong and I busted my shoulder. That was the last time I worked in the business. You know something? Helen Jerome was the only one to send a message to the hospital. She sent me a bottle of booze and a card. "Get well, we need you".' He shook his head sadly. 'Only they didn't.'

We went back inside. I felt relaxed for the first time. We sat for a while, drinking coffee and occasionally talking but mostly watching the movie.

Suddenly there was a man on the screen, reading a newsflash. He announced the death of Vernon Duke. I listened carefully but they were being cagey, either that or the cause of death hadn't been released.

I said goodbye to Brad, then went out to the Bentley. On the off-chance that Lieutenant Bercovici was still at her office being grilled by the Chief I used the payphone and called her. She was there and bursting to ask questions but I think she was afraid what the answers might be.

'You got the tape I sent?' I asked.

'Yes. What did . . ?' She stopped.

'Did you get McQuaid?'

'He was trying to dig up the landline. Did you . . ?' Again she changed her mind and stopped in mid-question.

'How about our friend, any sign of him?'

I didn't need to tell her I was talking about Corelli. 'No sign of him anywhere. He's either dropped through a hole in the ground or he's left town. My guess is he's on his way back east.'

I wasn't so sure about that but I didn't say so. 'How long will you be tied up?' I asked instead.

'Nearly through. Things haven't worked out too bad. It

seems the Chief kind of hoped you and I might do what we did which is why he let you have plenty of rope and why I was suspended.'

'Then you've got your job back?'

'Yes.'

I didn't feel as happy about that as the lieutenant sounded. 'I have to take Helen Jerome's car back,' I told her.

'Won't it keep for a while?'

'Of course, it will. I'll go back to your place now.'

I did as I promised and when the lieutenant showed up about an hour later I was already in bed and waiting.

'Are you trying to tell me something?' she asked as she came into the bedroom.

I grinned at her. 'You talk too much.'

So she stopped talking and so did I although for the next hour or more we made a lot of noise. It was that kind of lovemaking.

'Now what?' the lieutenant asked when we eventually stopped because the flesh was proving momentarily weaker than the spirit.

'You're insatiable,' I said. 'I was hoping for a breathing space.'

She kissed me lightly. 'I didn't mean that. What are you planning to do with the rest of your time here?'

'I promised to go to the movies with a beautiful lady,' I told her.

She leaned over me, not quite angry. 'Who?'

'A movie star.'

Her expression lightened. 'Helen Jerome?'

'Yes.'

'That I will allow.'

'And I want to make sure Linda is okay, maybe Barbara too.'

'Linda I agree to, I'm not so sure about the other one.

You were just a little too close for comfort.'

"Don't worry, you're safe.'

'It's not me I'm worrying about.'

'I also went to see Bill Berry and his son and find some way to thank them for helping me find Linda, and after that I plan to drive north. My return flight is from San Francisco.'

'You could change it and fly back from here.'

'I was thinking of going up to Bodega Bay.'

'Bodega Bay is for the birds.'

I laughed. For a few moments we lay silent, my arms around her. 'Have you any leave coming?' I asked.

'I thought you'd never ask.'

'Then you have?'

'A few days but I think the Chief might let me stretch it out a little.' Turning towards me she blew aside a strand of hair that had fallen across her cheek. 'Remember I said my daughter was in Oregon? Well, I thought I might drive up to collect her.'

'And the route to Oregon passes through San Francisco.'

'It even passes through Bodega Bay.'

'I think we have a deal, Lieutenant. Provided one thing.'

'What's that?'

I ran my hands down her naked body, tracing the soft moulded contours that already I knew better than any woman I'd ever known in the past, not excluding my wife. 'I think it's high time I knew your first name,' I said.

'Victoria.'

'Mm. Very stately.'

'Not Vicky,' she warned.

'I wouldn't dream of it.' I slid out of her embrace and stood up.

'Where are you going?'

'I am suddenly very hungry and if we are to do what I have planned for the next few hours I will need all my strength.'

'What do you plan?' she asked.

I leered. 'Use your imagination while I'm downstairs and I'll bet a month's pay you don't get even half of it.'

She put her hands behind her head and smiled at me. The posture did a great deal for her breasts and my blood pressure. 'Don't count on it,' she said.

I put on pants and a shirt and went down to the kitchen. I broke eggs into a bowl, then found mushrooms and tomatoes. I was working over them, slicing them neatly with an extra sharp knife when a I heard a tiny sound behind me. 'Decided you couldn't bear being without me?' I asked and glanced over my shoulder.

I froze.

Victoria was standing just inside the kitchen door, completely naked, as I'd left her. Behind her stood Corelli. One arm encircling her body, the fingers of his hand digging into her right breast. In his other hand he held a gun and it was pushed hard into her neck just below the ear.

'You fixed me, Mace,' he said, his eyes glittering beneath his heavy, scarred brows. 'Both of you did, and now it's my turn.'

I started breathing again, but shallowly. I still hadn't moved my body, only my head was turned. I held the knife in my hand and he couldn't have seen it although if he chose to think about what I was doing in the kitchen he might soon guess.

'Run out of hit-men?' I asked, trying to keep my voice casual.

'I had this whole state ready for plucking,' he said. 'Me, not the other two-bit characters with the family connections. I would've overruled them all. Only you fixed it so that not only is Vernon Duke off the hook, I'm being fingered for causing trouble with the cops and with the government.'

So he was a target. His own people had decided he'd outlived his usefulness. I couldn't feel anything except that in their own peculiar, misbegotten way, the organisation he worked for had come around to thinking like me. Corelli had to die.

I was turning the knife now, holding it by the blade.

I looked at Victoria. Her eyes were on me. I read a thousand messages in them. Corelli's fingers had turned her breast white where they squeezed.

I had never thrown a knife. Even if I had done so, this was no carefully balanced and flighted throwing knife. It was just a kitchen utensil, something used for cutting up vegetables.

And even if I was a knife-thrower of circus-tent standard, only part of the target was visible behind Victoria's flawless body.

'Leave her alone, Corelli,' I said. 'All she did was her job.'

'Leave her alone? The hell I will, Mace. She dies, and believe me, when she does she'll welcome it.'

His fingers tightened savagely into Victoria's breast. The action made her gasp with pain and her body twisted convulsively to the right.

It wasn't much of a movement, but it revealed a few extra inches of Corelli's body. I didn't take time to think about the possible consequences because I knew that thin as the chances was, it was the only one I was likely to have.

I threw the knife.

If there is a special saint somewhere who looks after policemen and policewomen he, or she, was on duty at that moment.

The point of the knife hit Corelli square in the throat, slicing through skin and gristle as it opened up his windpipe.

The gun went off but the bullet smashed harmlessly into the ceiling.

Then I was across the room, snatching the gun away with one hand and pulling Victoria to me with the other.

I hadn't needed to take the gun. There was nothing left to pull the trigger again, not even a dying twitch of a nerve.

Corelli was sliding down the wall behind him, blood gushing out and all over Victoria's body and legs. I threw the gun to one side, picked her up, and carried her out of there.

I stood with her under the shower, holding her and washing away the blood. It didn't matter that my clothes were sodden, the only thing that did matter was that she was unharmed.

Afterwards, I lay her on the bed, covered her with a sheet, trying not to look at the bright red weals where Corelli's fingers had dug into her flesh, and told her to stay there while I did what had to be done.

I called her Chief. It was time we heard each other's voice and I knew this wasn't a situation for anyone but him to handle.

Until he arrived I stayed upstairs, holding her hand and gently caressing her face with my lips. But she was tougher than I liked to pretend and when we heard the Chief's car arrive outside she told me to get the hell out of there and to stop treating her as though she were a child.

It took a while to do what had to be done and the Chief proved surprisingly amenable to having someone come in and tidy up the house while the lieutenant and I went out.

I took her with me when I returned Helen Jerome's Bentley and we held hands as we watched *Countess from Chicago* with the old star. Just before we left the house in Vedado Avenue Helen whispered to me that she wasn't really jealous and that she thought we made an excellent couple. I told her about the owner of the bar who was an old fan and former stuntman and she remembered him and promised to go and see him soon. I was pleased about that, not that I thought I was playing Cupid but maybe she would enjoy talking to someone who wasn't yet ready for Forest Lawns but who could share in her recollections of the old days.

Lieutenant Bercovici and I stayed close the next day too, as I talked with Linda and Bill Berry and his family and then we took her car and spent the rest of my holiday driving north to San Francisco. It was a week that should have lasted forever.

It would be nice to say how much I enjoyed the scenery but the truth is I didn't look at much else beside her. And one motel room was much like another, once we were in bed.

We never did make it all the way up to Bodega Bay but as we said goodbye at the airport, after my flight had been called, she kissed me one last time and told me all the things we had yet to do. Bodega Bay was only one of them, and was far from the most interesting.

'Be careful.' I told her. 'Your town's a dangerous place.'

'It wasn't so bad before you arrived.'

We looked at one another, long and searchingly. The memory of this moment would have to last quite a while and we both knew it.

'Tell me something, Mace,' Victoria said. 'What's your first name?'

I grinned. 'I don't know you well enough for that yet.'

'Damn you for a stubborn bastard.'

'I try my best.'

'Then tell me something else.'

'What?'

'Will you come back?'

I smiled and kissed the tip of her nose. 'I'll be back,' I promised.

And I will.

